I0656480

Footprints of the Outsider

Julius Ocwinyo

Fountain Publishers

Fountain Publishers
P.O. Box 488
Kampala
Email: fountain@starcom.co.ug
Website: www.fountain publishers.com

ISBN 9970 02 343 8

Dedication

To you
Fr Pietro Foletto
My first mentor
In things literary
and you
Geoffrey Angela
Who helped me
More than
You will ever know:
To both of you
 I dedicate
This modest product
Of another attempt.

❧

Apac District

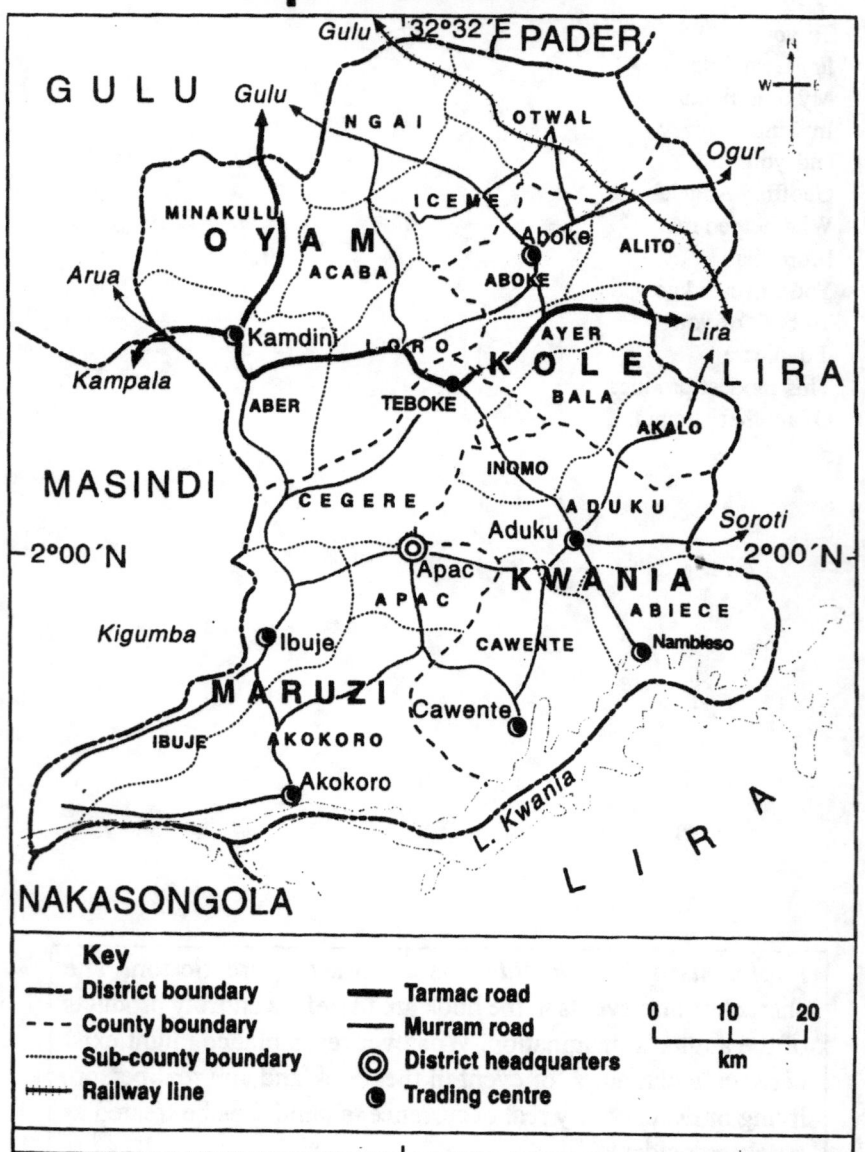

Chapter I

Sometimes one's destiny is decided by the nature of one's birth. Sometimes the moment of one's birth plays a crucial part too. Often, however, things happen to a person that make him wonder whether nature or moment of birth had anything to do with it. That, perhaps, is the only justification for telling this story.

This is largely the story of Abudu Olwit, who might be a member of parliament now, or who might not. It is also the story of Teboke, the village with a not-so-long history where he was born and where he was mostly raised.

Abudu Olwit was born in a little mud-walled hut with a thatch roof riddled with holes. Apart from his mother, Alicinora, the only person present at his birth was Akaci, the local midwife. After binding Olwit's umbilical cord with sisal string and cutting it with an old Nacet safety razor, Akaci gently dipped him in a patched metal basin half-full of tepid swamp water and bathed him without soap.

When Abudu Olwit was born, Teboke seemed set to become the nerve-centre of Cegere sub-county. Two Indians, Hippen and Ramchand, had arrived there a few years before and proceeded to plant a cotton ginnery right in its centre. They had then constructed a tall concrete tower and mounted a siren upon its top. Every morning this siren shattered the air with its strident scream that summoned one shift to work and dismissed another. The ginnery machines clanked and clattered and rasped and whooshed all day and all night, every day.

The two Indians were a very wily lot. They recruited most of their workers from among far-off tribes. They knew how difficult it was for a man who came from so far away in the hope of making enough money to be able to afford a wife, or to buy a bicycle, to go back to his home village without it. For he would at once become the laughing-stock of the whole village. And no sane man would want that to happen to him.

The Indians recruited mostly in the north-west and north-east of the country. They recruited from among the Madi, the Lugbara and the Kakwa, and from among the Jabwor. They also hired those

1

Karimojong who were too cowardly to go on cattle raids, and who were therefore despised and shunned by their own tribespeople. They made forays among the refugees too, hiring mostly Sudanese, but hardly ever Congolese. The Congolese, the Indians seemed to believe, were too steeped in music to be of much use in a ginnery. They did not ignore the locals entirely though, but hired very few of them. Even if the Indians had wanted to recruit many more of the local men than presented themselves for hire, it would not have been possible, for most of them despised the manual types of ginnery work, considering them inferior to peasant farming.

The men whom the Indians recruited from the north-east and north-west of the country, and from Teboke itself, worked on the ginnery floor. They ginned the cotton, moved it about, baled it. Or they fed the big logs into the boiler furnace to keep the steam up. The Indians paid these men very little money, mostly in hole-centred coins. They, however, ensured that the men were kept constantly in food, so that though their pay was barely enough to take care of their most basic needs, they always had something to eat – even if it was only dried beans and maize flour most of the time.

And the Indians would scream at them above the deafening noise of the ginnery machines, in bad Swahili:

'Boyi, kuja hapa!	(Boy, come here!)
'Boyi, nataka nini?'	(Boy, what do you want?)
'Boyi, kama wewe hapana	(Boy, if you do not do the
fanya kazi mzuri, si mpa pesa	work properly, I will not
yao!'	pay you!)
'Boooyii...!!'	(Boy....!!)

Sometimes the Indians chose, as their workers milled around during the one-hour lunch break, to toss a few coins among them. The ginnery workers would scramble for the coins, dropping down and fighting as if for a most precious prize. And the Indians would speak in high-pitched Gujarati voices and laugh ha! ha! ha! haw! haw! haw! hoo! hoo! hoo!

Teboke folks considered the ginnery workers recruited from afar to be a breed of men different from themselves. They did not think they were special in any way, yet they were not quite equal, for they were men trucked in from other parts of the country, men who spoke alien tongues comprehensible only among themselves. Furthermore, their lives were intimately linked to the clanking, whining, panting, grinding machines that turned the heavily-seeded cotton into soft and beautiful lint, and that pressed the lint into rock-hard bales which would then be trucked to distant, unknown places.

These ginnery workers belonged, yet did not quite belong in Teboke. They lived among the locals, yet they did not own any of the land. And a man without land could at best be deemed to be only half a man. The ginnery workers were quite often, however, good, hardworking, honest folk who were not averse to standing a few drinks for the locals every now and then. Sometimes, too, they took up with those of the local girls who, for one reason or another, none of the local men would want to be seen hovering around –and made the girls' mothers proud. Nobody could ask more of a neighbour, even if he were a foreigner, such as these men were.

There was, however, a difference between the origins of the men who worked on the ginnery floor and those who did the paperwork. For the men who did the paperwork, the Indians cast their eyes southwards. It was in this direction that they sought the accountant, the clerks and the cashier. There was, for example, an 'Ikangi'. To this day, no-one is sure how it should be spelt: Ikangi, Ikanggi, Ekangi, or Ikaangi. The reason was that they were more interested in the way the name rolled off the tongue than in how it sat on paper. In any case, few of them had learnt to read and write.

The people of Teboke were deeply interested in Ikangi's origins, and in his daughters. In every Teboke home people conjectured. Some said he was an *Anyoro*, with others insisting that he was actually brother to that famous Nyoro king, Kabalega, for the job he held, they stressed, was one fit for the brother of a *mukama*, a king. Others insisted he was an *Aganna*, for was it not that Muganda, Kakungulu, who had brought the white man's ways and things to Lango? Would it therefore be far-fetched to believe that Ikangi was Kakungulu's own son, even though he worked for Indians? Still others

3

insisted he was a *mubulisi*, one of those mysterious inhabitants of the Kenyan coast that was said to crawl with sly and softly-seductive spirit-beings that were half-woman, half-fish. Otherwise how could one explain his very light skin? Furthermore, a *mubulisi* had a short, hairy tail. Now if Ikangi did not have a short tail himself, why did he not go swimming in Okole swamp like other men? And why did he always have his bath inside his large, sprawling house instead of in an outdoor bath shelter, like other folk? Did he perhaps fear that someone might peep through a crack in the walls of the bath shelter and see his short, hairy tail?

Tail or no tail, no-one doubted that Ikangi was of royal, or semi-royal, blood, that he was either a direct descendant of, or a close relative to, some *abaka* or other . An *abaka* was a *rwot adit,* a big chief, so anyone who was even remotely related to him by blood had to be some kind of *rwot*, chief! No, Ikangi was not an *akopi*, a commoner; there was no way he could be one!

Few people in Teboke knew exactly what Ikangi's job in the ginnery was, but everyone was certain that his presence was very important for the running of the ginnery. Even the huffing, smoking, steaming, whirring ginnery acknowledged this, for some of its machines sang:

Yoo tung Ikangi	Where is the road
Tye kwene?	To Ikangi's home?
Yoo tung Ikangi	Where is the road
Tye kwene?	To Ikangi's home?
Yoo tung Ikangi	Where is the road
Tye kwene?	To Ikangi's home?

And others responded, in counterpoint:

En ien!	It is here!
En ien!	It is here!
En ien!	It is here!

The machines sang thus, day in, day out, without let-up. Now if the white main's machines felt that it was important enough for

4

everyone to know the way to Ikangi's home, then Ikangi himself had to be a very important person indeed!

It was whispered that, when construction of the ginnery had been completed, the Indians had commissioned Ikangi to abduct any young boy with a bulging navel so that his neck could be slit and his blood splashed on the ginnery machines. This blood-libation, they said, would ensure that the machines ran without trouble.

It was also whispered that Ikangi was a Yellow Fever. A Yellow Fever was one of those men who drove around in their cars at night in search of people to kidnap and send to Entebbe. With the headlights of a Yellow Fever's car switched off and the car just crawling along, the Yellow Fever would fling a noose around the neck of his intended victim and drag him into the car. Inside the car the victim would be injected through a huge hypodermic needle with a drug that numbed his body and made him behave like an idiot. The Yellow Fever would then take his captive to Entebbe, where he would be paid a large amount of money. The captive would never be seen or heard of again.

Ikangi was a very mysterious man indeed, and he was deeply feared.

As for Ikangi's daughters, they were the kind of daughters a father would demand a lot of bridewealth for because they counted among the most beautiful girls in Teboke. It was said of them that they were human lamps, for they made a place shine with their presence. Even a mere glimpse of them made a man's eyes light up with lust.

Ikangi's daughters had the most delicate limbs in Teboke. Also some of the broadest hips and longest necks, necks which the locals loved to compare with that of the *aniem* antelope. Their skin was so light that you could almost see the veins underneath them. The only girls of local extraction who were blessed with such delicate skin were Kurucita's daughters, but then they did not seem to match Ikangi's daughters in grace and elegance, not quite.

Ikangi's daughters were also very haughty. When they swung gracefully past the local men, their eyes dimmed to an inscrutable slate with unseeing. They hardly ever greeted the men. The men hungered for them, even if they inwardly told themselves – and each

5

other, openly – that they did not exactly care for the girls, for were they not *olaya*, girls of loose morals? Yet the men's hearts grew parched with longing for the girls, for is it not true that while the mouth can very easily be made to lie, the heart will always tell the truth – the whole, plain, hurtful extent of it – to the man who carries it within himself? Each time the girls swayed past these men without so much as giving them a smile or a nod of recognition, therefore, they felt a little hurt, a little diminished. But still they went on hoping. This hoping, however, did not stop them saying all sorts of vile, outrageous things about the girls, while praying all the while that they should both get pregnant out of wedlock, for was there a curse worse than this, except perhaps the curse of leprosy? Was it not known that a girl who fell pregnant while still living in her father's compound lost so much of her worth that she would thereafter be willing to sleep with anybody, even a leper?

The cotton that was ginned at the ginnery that Ikangi helped the Indians run was brought in on timbery Morris and Bedford trucks. These trucks had windows furnished with rectangular pieces of strong brown canvas. When it was not raining , or when the air was not very dusty, the pieces of canvas were rolled up and fastened to the roof of the driver's cabin. When it began to rain, or when it got too dusty for the driver's comfort, the canvas covers were let down and latched to the window sills. There was a little square patch of transparent material in the centre of the canvas covers through which the driver could peep outside.

People were always awed by the way the engines of the trucks were set in motion. All the drivers seemed to go about it the same way. They would push one end of the angled crank into the hole in the steel bumper, roll up their shirtsleeves – even when they were short–, spray fine spittle on their palms, rub them together. Then they would firmly grip the free end of the crank and jerk away. Up–down; up–down; up, down; up, down; up–down, up–down, up–down, up-down, up-down... The engines would at first cough and convulse like a medium conjuring up the spirit of somebody long dead. Then they would gurgle and roar into seemingly unquenchable life. This would set the trucks shuddering from nose to tail, as if they were in the grip of a vengeful ancestral spirit. It was at this moment that the

6

drivers would leap up, crank in hand, bound round the front of the trucks, past the fat mudguards, yank the flat, plain cab door open and leap onto the bench seat. They would then noisily mesh the gears and drive thunderously away.

Some of the trucks were of the flatbed type, and these sometimes collected the cotton from the primary cooperative society stores. Once the cotton was tied up in large sheets of sacking and loaded onto the trucks, it would be fastened down with thick, strong sisal ropes passed around hooks screwed into the sides of the truck bed. Then those travelling with the cotton to the ginnery would scramble up the large mounds of cotton and perch themselves on top of the load. Thereafter the trucks would be on their way, with the drivers often paying scant attention to the plight of the dust-covered humans bouncing precariously about behind their clattering cabin.

The two roads that led into, and therefore out of, Teboke were built under the white man's rule.

One road ran due north-east. If you followed it you would pass through Loro, Acaba, Ngai, Bobi and on to the lands of the Acholi, the Alur, the Madi, and the Lugbara. It was said that this road led to Sudan, the land of lanky, ant-black sorghum eaters, and to Congo, the land of dog-and-python-eating magicians.

It had taken the white man a great deal of trouble to get this road built. The whites seemed to believe that the only way to get a Lango man to work for them was to whip him. So the whites who supervised the construction of the road – and other roads in Lango as well – used the hippo-hide whip very liberally. The result was that the road was completed in record time.

Now the Teboke-Loro road had two steel-and-concrete bridges, Abam Adwong and Abam Atidi, fitted with steel guard rails at both edges, and the waters of Okole swamp swished, gurgled and bubbled merrily under the bridges and through the many steel culverts on their long journey south.

Stories were often told of the considerable number of men who lost their lives to hippos in Okole swamp as they built the road across it. The most dangerous part of the swamp was a very clear stretch of water called Arau-Okun, 'The Place Where Hippos Sulk'. It was at Arau-Okun that many of the men lost their lives.

7

It was a very tragic occurrence indeed when a hippo bit a man. Hippos had the frightening inclination to bite people around the middle, neatly cleaving them into two. The horrible thing about it all was that the victim of a hippo-bite never stopped talking, even in death. He would keep on chanting:

> If I had not outrun that hippo
> I would be dead by now...

> If I had not outrun that hippo
> I would be dead by now...

> If I had not outrun that hippo
> I would be dead by now...

On and on and on and on...

The only way to get the head of a hippo-bite victim to shut up was to tap it lightly with a spear-shaft. Then the head would promptly fall silent, dying properly at last.

The second road that led into, and out of, Teboke ran due northeast towards Lira town. It crept brown, narrow and sinuous through Alee, Lwala, Alemi and other big and small trading centres. The Kampala-bound buses travelled this road, moving southwards away from Lira town and passing through Loro, Atura, Masindi Port, then on through the land of the Baganda to Kampala, the capital city. The heavy trucks from Mombasa and such far-off places also plied this road. Many of the Teboke folks wondered how the drivers of the trucks from Mombasa survived the sorcery and witchcraft of Mombasa, how they avoided being carried away and drowned by those wicked female fish-humans that prowled Mombasa with the stealth of wizards. The truck drivers were a very promiscuous lot, so if the fish-humans had vanished with them to the bottom of those waters that were said to be many times larger and deeper than Arau-Okun, the abode of the man-cutting hippos, no-one would have been surprised at all.

Every day, all tribes of cars, lorries and buses tumbled into Teboke along this road – the small and the big, the new and the old, those that let off a light sickly-sweet smoke and those that belched out black, acrid smoke. Sometimes after a vehicle had passed and the dust it had raised had settled, the children of Teboke would rush into the road and scoop up a little soil from it. They would proceed to mix the soil with some sugar and then eat it. They claimed that the sugar tasted better that way.

Sometimes the rain fell long and thick and heavy, and it turned the road into a thick, treacherous paste. Buses, trucks and cars frequently got stuck in this sludge. Then the people of Teboke would be excited and deeply happy, for whenever a vehicle got stuck its driver had to turn to the locals to help him get out of his predicament. And the locals would ask to be paid.

It was even better when a diesel tanker truck got stuck and keeled over, for quite often the fuel inside its large belly would come gushing out and the locals would catch it in their *debes* and basins and pails and bowls and even cups, and use it in their lamps. They did not need to worry that the diesel tankers would follow another route next time, for there was no other route to follow: the Lira-Kampala tarmac road that would make travel so much more comfortable and easy had not yet been built.

So the vehicles went on getting stuck, sometimes for hours, even days, whenever the rains visited.

Stories were often told of a man whose feet got stuck in the mud along the stretch that marks the boundary between Teboke and Alee village. It was around midnight when this was supposed to have happened. The man, it was said, was returning to Alee from drinking *arege* gin at Teboke trading centre. He was said to have been so drunk that if he had touched his anus he would have mistaken it for a mere scar. When the stodgy mud gripped his feet, he was belting out his *arege* praise-song in English:

Arege white water
Oh *arege*
You tough water

Oh *arege*
Widout you I don know
What I will do
Oh *arege*
I lab' you more dan
Any woman I met
Oh *arege*

When the mud gripped his feet, the song promptly withered on his lips. Ex-soldier though he was, he was deeply frightened, not least because the spot where he was stuck was very close to a large, bushy *itek* tree believed to be the abode of malevolent spirits. It was said that these spirits sometimes attacked drunkards at night, lashing them so heavily with stinging *opobo* sticks that the following day it would be next to impossible to recognise their victims, for their bodies would be covered from head to toe in *opobo*-induced weals. So the frightened Uganda Army veteran had to stay put right there in the middle of the road until morning, before he could be rescued. Such was the clutching power of the mud.

It was around this time, five years before construction of the Lira-Kampala tarmac and two years before president Bwete abolished Uganda's kingdoms, that Abudu was born. Not that Abudu was a Muslim. What happened was that his mother, Alicinora, having slept with many different men during the month she first missed her period, had decided that she liked one of her lovers, Musa Wangolo the Mugisu, the most. Musa Wangolo was one of the few people not from northern Uganda who worked at the ginnery. Whenever he was not dragging bales around the ginnery floor, he fetched water for the Arab shopkeepers. Since Musa Wangolo was a Muslim, Alicinora deemed it fitting for her to award her son a decent Muslim name, Abudu.

Abudu's mother was an *alaya*, a woman of easy virtue. Men liked comparing her to *icwica*, the leaves of the pumpkin plant, the cheapest and most easily available food in Lango, food that becomes particularly useful in times of famine. Alicinora was a woman to whom a man turned when there was no other woman available to take.

10

Alicinora was very dark, and she hated her colour. She was squat and fat and rough-skinned, and her eyes seemed to be permanently bloodshot. She also possessed a particularly crude and peppery tongue. And she always worried: I am short and rough-skinned and ugly. If only I was beautiful!

When Abudu Olwit was conceived, Alicinora was twenty-three and had just had her eleventh infection of syphilis treated. She was no stranger to this disease, for it had become a frequent visitor to her since she first caught it at the tender age of thirteen. Abudu Olwit would be Alicinora's only child, and when he grew up would marry a young woman called Saida Acola.

At the time of Saida Acola's birth Abudu Olwit had lived through seven wet and seven dry seasons. The stool of national power had been snatched from Bwete a little more than a year earlier. The new occupant of the presidential stool was a burly army general who had started out as a private in *kea*, the British colonial army. He was called Idi.

Saida Acola's mother, Bitoroci Alupu, was the wife of a sub-county chief, a *jago*. When Bitoroci talked, her throat throbbed like that of a male lizard. It was said of her that if she had been a tree, no-one would have dared rest in her shade, for her lashing and malicious tongue offered people little comfort. Her unpleasant disposition was worsened by a nagging suspicion on her part that no-one meant well by her because of her exalted position as the favourite wife of her chiefly husband. She believed that that was one reason why her second child, a boy, had died of stiff-neck disease. Somebody who envied her had sent the disease to kill her son. If that was not the case, why had the little boy not responded to all the herbs and poultices and barks and powders that she had administered to him? She had even fed him a whole bottle of Masurubu liniment to no avail!

Saida Acola's father, *Jago* Olima, was forty-eight years old when he married Bitoroci, who had turned nineteen barely a month earlier. *Jago* Olima owned around three hundred head of cattle and his home therefore reeked with milk and ghee. He also owned a hunting rifle and shotgun with which he put paid to many sitatunga and buffalo and hippo and waterbuck and duiker and guinea fowl. As a result

11

he fed his children, wives and relatives on a lot of bushmeat. This, however, only lasted up to the removal of president Bwete, for when Idi slumped his bulk on the seat of power, he stopped the use of firearms by everybody else except the members of his own armed forces.

The animals that *Jago* Olima had killed, however, were said to haunt him. Especially the buffaloes and hippos. Their *orongo* ghosts would enter him quite frequently and drive him mad. Whenever he was in the grip of the animal-ghosts he would rush around screaming and attacking people. When Olima was in this state, it frequently required no fewer than ten strong men to subdue him and tie him up. He would then be taken to a medicine man who would exorcise the ghosts. The animal-ghosts would enter him sooner or later again, and he would have to be tied up and taken to a medicine man for yet another round of exorcism. Once an animal was angry with you for taking its life, it was believed, it never left you alone, especially if it was a hippo, a buffalo or an elephant.

Olima had become a sub-county chief when he was barely thirty. Within ten years he had married five young wives. Before Saida Acola's mother had come along eighteen years after Olima's appointment as sub-county chief, Olima had taken another two young women to wife. When he married Saida Acola's mother, however, three of his wives had departed. The year Acola was born, therefore, Olima was the proud and respected husband of five women, including Acola's mother, Bitoroci.

Jago Olima possessed a big home in Teboke where two of his wives lived. One of these wives was Bitoroci.

Chapter II

A Bachelor of Arts degree was not a small thing. Especially if it came from Makerere University. And Abudu Owit was the proud owner of one – a BA(Econ).

Abudu Olwit had entered Makerere University when it was the only university in Uganda. He had in fact joined Makerere twice, the first time to study for a diploma in Music, Dance and Drama, and the second time to do his BA(Econ). What changed Olwit's mind about the Music, Dance and Drama course was what people thought about it. In Teboke they said that he had gone to Makerere University to learn how to dance and sing, so Teboke showed him little respect. At the university itself they called him Olwit *musiru ddala ddala* – 'very, very stupid'. The *musiru ddala ddala* came from the abbreviation of Music, Dance and Drama – MDD – and it applied to all his course mates too. Before he could complete the course, Olwit did not want to be associated with it any more, so he decided to re-sit A levels, from within the precincts of Makerere University. He did the exams well enough to be re-admitted there, but this time for another course, BA (Econ). Not that Olwit had wanted to read Economics as such, but all he wanted was a degree in something that sounded impressive, and Economics was one such discipline. So he opted for a BA (Econ) degree.

When Olwit had been admitted for the Music, Dance and Drama course, his maternal uncle, Odwong, had found it very difficult to understand that one could be taught to sing, dance and play at university, even at Makerere.

'My son,' Odwong told Olwit when he had been told about the course . He always addressed Olwit as 'my son' and treated him as one. 'Tell me, my son, what is this I hear about your going to university to learn to sing, dance and play?'

Olwit was not taken aback at all. Instead he was amused, and the amusement showed on his face. His uncle, he knew, had learnt about the course from people who were as underexposed to the things and ways of the modern world as the uncle himself, and who were therefore as mystified. Olwit tried to explain.

'Uncle,' he said, 'the course is not really about singing, dancing and playing as you put it... But first of all, who told you? I do not remember telling you.'

'I heard about it at the trading centre. Teboke trading centre, that is, not Alemi.' Odwong lived in Alemi trading centre and Olwit was visiting him. 'A lot of people in Teboke know about it. And they laugh about it, they laugh at you. They say that whereas other people's sons are going to Makerere to learn how to treat people, to repair planes, to become livestock doctors and to govern others, all you will learn is how to sing the white man's songs and do his dances. They also say that you will learn the dances and songs of the *onami* and how to pretend to be somebody else on a platform.' His uncle looked genuinely worried.

'That is not quite true, uncle,' Olwit said, trying to reassure his uncle. 'Look, I will learn how to write songs using the kind of writing meant for songs. I will...'

'You mean,' his uncle interrupted, his forehead wrinkling with puzzlement, 'you mean to say that you do not know how to write songs yet? Opio Ikoce, you know Opio Ikoce of course, don't you?'

'I know Opio Ikoce very well. Who does not know Opio Ikoce?'

'So you do! That is good.' Odwong was visibly excited. 'Whenever Opio Ikoce wakes up of a morning with a new song troubling his head, he does not bother to write it down though he can write. He went up to Junior Two, unlike me who dropped out in Standard Five... Well, I was saying that Opio Ikoce will first sing his song at a beer gathering to see if people like it, and then he will write it down later. The words of the song, that is what I am talking about.'

'No, that is not what I was talking about, uncle,' Olwit said, wondering whether he would ever be able to make his uncle understand. 'There is a difference between what I will do after my course and what Opio Ikoce does. It is like the difference between medicine men and hospital doctors. Medicine men do not have to be trained using books but hospital doctors have to read very many books. Yet both types of doctor treat people.'

'I do not quite understand. You have been learning the white man's songs right from the time you first went to school. I remember one of the first songs you sang to us. *I have seen a small girl s'e nather Jane.* And you sang it very well too. Do you really need to learn more songs, even if it means being able to write them in song language? Now when you get your *digiri* in singing and dancing, what job will the government give you?'

Olwit's uncle did not look angry. Yes, there was disappointment on his face. And confusion. But not anger. There was no anger on his face at all. All his face showed was a kind of blank bafflement.

If there was anybody his uncle was proud of, it was him. His uncle bragged about him frequently, and openly too. In the crop fields when he and his fellow peasants were engaged in communal digging. At drinking places when the fumes of *arege* had filled his head. At Alemi trading centre where he liked playing the board game, *coro.* Even in Lwala swamp where, during the dry season when the level of water had dropped, he went to take part in the communal fish-hunt. He was known, on a number of occasions, to have exploded into a very loud praise-chant when he speared a fish, especially if it was a very big lungfish. On each occasion he shouted:

Olwit kwani!	Olwit study hard!
Olwit kwan agwa!	Olwit excel in school!
An anekko rec!	I am killing fish!
Anekko rec adongo!	Killing big fish!
Rec adongo apol!	Many big fish!
Anekko rec	Killing fish
Ate culi piji!	To pay your fees!

But how could he make his uncle see the possibilities that lay in such a course as Music, Dance and Drama? How could he convince him that learning to sing and write songs, to dance and make believe was not all there was to the course? How could he convince him that it was not only with the government that one could find a job? He could, together with others, set up his own theatre group, couldn't he? But would his uncle be able to understand this? Would other people be able to understand this?

Olwit was very much aware of the kinds of people parents wanted their children to emulate: lawyers, administrators, politicians, medical doctors, vet doctors, headteachers, medical assistants, pastors, bus drivers, truck drivers... How would he fit in, he who would probably strike out in an entirely unfamiliar direction?

'Uncle,' Olwit said, 'it is not only the government that provides jobs. One can get a job elsewhere. One can even create one's own job. It is possible.'

'Olwit... Olwit my child,' Odwong said, cocking his head to one side and looking at Olwit with eyes filled with pity, 'you are still young, my child, that is why you talk such talk. It is not easy to create a job. In any case, if you did not want a government job, then why did you stay in school for so long, even finishing senior?'

'Look, uncle, I –' Olwit said. His eyes pleaded for understanding.

'Hear me out first, my child,' Odwong interrupted. 'Look at all the important people we see around here. Look at how people respect them. Do you not want to be like them? The politicians, for example. You know how our own member of parliament, Adoli-Awal, is treated. Whenever he passes through here, big crowds collect around him. People clap for him, they compose songs that praise him. When women look at him, you can see the desire in their eyes. People envy the MP. They envy him his suits, his car, his shoes, his friends. Would you not like to be treated in the same way, my son?'

'But uncle, not everyone can be an MP,' Olwit responded, his voice low and hoarse.

'You speak the truth, son,' Odwong responded, speaking slowly. 'Not everyone can become an MP. I am not saying that you will become one today or tomorrow. In the first place, you do not have the money. And not many people know you. But could you not try for something better than a singer and dancer? For instance, a District Commissioner or a magistrate? After all some of these District Commissioners do not even possess *digiri*. Akeny, for example, has only a Grade Three teacher's certificate. So if you could acquire a *digiri* in something else, rather than in singing and dancing...'

Then Olwit made the mistake of telling Odwong that Music, Dance and Drama was not even a degree course.

'What?' Odwong exclaimed and closed his eyes. 'What did you say? You are going to make me weep.' Then he opened his eyes

16

and shook his head, slowly. 'My son, I hope they are not going to give you a *catabiket* when you finish?'

'No, it is not a certificate. It is a diploma.' Odwong closed his eyes tight again, shook his head briskly. Then he opened his eyes.

'My child,' he said, at last, ' I think it would make no sense for you to go to Makerere to acquire only a diploma. Why don't you go elsewhere instead and do a proper course? Look at Walter Ongom, for example, who got his diploma from Busita Agricultural College. Look at the beautiful motorcycle he rides. Look how proud he is, how much he is admired!'

When will people's attitudes change? Olwit wondered. Why do they often admire – even adore–people who, because of the jobs or positions they hold, are frequently inclined to look down on them, deride them, even intimidate them? Had Odwong himself not told him about a minor politician who had visited their primary school only a few months after the white man had put Uganda back in the hands of its black owners? His uncle had been fifteen then and in Standard Five – as Primary Five was called then. In a class where about half the pupils were already grown men, some having started school at fifteen or sixteen, Odwong had been one of the youngest 'children' in the class.

The minor politician had arrived in a sleek, black Mercedes Benz from the direction of Loro in the north-west. The school had erected an arch of elephant-grass reeds in his honour at the spot where the road from Loro met the one from Corner Ayer. From that point up to where the visitor would turn off into the school compound a number of young banana trees had been planted on both sides of the road. The school headmaster, in the company of some of his teachers and members of the school's management committee, had constituted themselves into a welcome committee and patiently awaited their guest's arrival. When the guest arrived, he got out and shook hands with all the members of the welcome committee. Then he got back into his sleek, black Benz. The Benz started moving again, crawling at near-tortoise speed so that the welcome committee could keep pace with it. When the Benz reached the middle of the compound the driver parked it under the group of mango trees in whose shade teachers often sat to plan their lessons and to mark their pupils' books.

When the guest stepped out, he was escorted to the Standard Seven classroom, a large room that sometimes served as an assembly hall, and sometimes as a dance hall. All the pupils had already assembled in this room, awaiting their guest's grand entry. The moment the guest appeared in the doorway all the pupils stood up and erupted into a song of welcome, their voices discordant and shrill with anxiety:

You are welcome
You are welcome
Our dear visitah!

We are proud
To receive you
Our dear visitah!

May God bless you
For visiting us
Our dear visitah!

Thank you for
Remembering us
Our dear visitah!

When the singing was over everybody sat down except the guest. Instead, he turned round to glare at the wooden office chair standing directly behind him. It was the kind of thinly cushioned, straight-backed chair very common in primary schools then. Contempt for the chair first curled the guest's lips before it mounted slowly up his face. Then the guest grabbed the chair by its back, lifted it about two feet off the floor, held it aloft for a few moments and then released it. It crashed back to the floor with a heavy clatter. Some of the pupils jumped, startled. After that he spoke, ignoring the teachers and members of the management committee seated beside him . He addressed himself directly to the pupils.

18

'I do not know what is wrong with some people,' he remarked. 'A very important person takes the trouble to visit you and you insult him by giving him a hard chair to sit on as if his buttocks were made of metal!' He wagged a finger in the pupils' faces. 'Let me tell you one thing. When I was first elected to my present post, the chair that I was offered was so soft that when I sat in it for the first time I sank in right up to my chest... And now they offer me a hard wooden chair to sit on. As if my buttocks were made of metal.'

Then he picked up the chair again, eyed it with disdain, and banged it back on the floor. After that he calmly folded his arms in front of his chest and – not sitting yet – arrowed a slit-eyed look at the headmaster.

The headmaster, who had sat paralysed right through this short speech, suddenly came alive, panicking. He left the room, running. A few minutes later he arrived back panting, carrying one of his better sofas with his wife. Together, the headmaster and his wife removed the chair from behind their guest and replaced it with the sofa, pushing it close enough to properly align it with his buttocks. The guest first tested the seat with his fat, stubby fingers to establish whether it was soft enough for his non-metallic backside. Then he sank into the sofa with a sigh, a smug and satisfied look spreading over his entire face soon after. The headmaster flashed an ingratiating smile at his guest and launched into his welcome speech.

Olwit felt that if that was the kind of 'importance' his uncle wanted – and expected – him to acquire, then he had better get ready for deep disappointment. Power, power of any kind, was sweet. And, like stolen honey, it never cloyed. But even if he had wanted power ardently enough – especially political power – to try for it, would he be able to attain it, would he ever?

Look at his own member of parliament, Mike Adoli-Awal, for example. The son of a county chief, pumpkin-leaf soup was alien to his tongue, and his back never knew the corrugated hardness of an unmattressed papyrus mat, nor his stomach the coarseness of a cheap blanket. After Mike Adoli-Awal had completed junior secondary in Luwero in Buganda, Petero Lwanga, under whose charge his father had placed him, had driven him in his small Ford Anglia car to Namilyango College where he had received a first-class education.

Then off he had gone to Makerere University College, and then on to the London School of Economics. Even before his return to Uganda, everybody knew that sooner or later he would take advantage of the immense influence of his family and try for political office.

What about he, Olwit? If he had not been rescued by his uncle, Odwong, where would he be now? Probably pushing hand-made luggage barrows in Lira town, or in Mbale, where his mother had told him his father came from.

'Olwit,' his mother had told him one day when he was six, 'your father was a very nice man. And very generous too. He came from Mbale. He was called Musa Wangolo.'

'Where is Mbale?' he had asked.

'In Bugisu,' she had replied.

'Where is Bugisu?'

'In another part of this country. Far away from here.'

'Why are we not there, living with my father?' His mother, seated on a papyrus mat shelling fresh pigeon peas, had shifted nervously.

'He would not take us with him,' she responded, then seemed to concentrate more on her shelling. 'Now go and play.'

'But –' he protested.

'Go and play, Olwit. I will tell you tomorrow,' she said firmly, her forehead furrowed.

Olwit went off to hunt lizards with the catapult slung around his neck.

His mother never told him about his father again. He was, however, to hear a lot about him later, especially from his fellow children, particularly when they wanted to put him down. They would call him *atin anam* – a foreigner's child – or *atin luk* – a bastard – , and frequently go on to describe the kind of man his father was and the circumstances under which he had been conceived. The more daring ones would call him, especially after he had fought them, *atin alaya* – a prostitute's child – and would sometimes spit on the ground – and very emphatically too–after addressing him thus. He had at first wondered about where such little boys had got all that information from, but when he had grown a little older, he had realised that his origins and his mother's scandalous behaviour was common

20

talk around Teboke and a number of the neighbouring villages. And it made him exceedingly angry.

Things had come to a head one day when he had been sent home from Amuka College for failure to pay his second-term fees. He was fifteen, and in Senior Two. He knew that his mother would not be able to raise the full fees balance, but he was tired of relying entirely on his uncle, Odwong, who had taken over the responsibility of educating him when he was in Primary Six. He believed that if his mother was determined, she could put up at least half the fees. She instead preferred to drink, and to booze up her lovers, past and present.

For example, her goings-on one Friday at Loro market had become part of Teboke folklore. It was said that she had distilled a full twenty-litre jerrycan of *arege*, which she then took to the weekly Friday market at Loro to sell. By the time about half of her *arege* had been bought, some of it on credit, she was already tipsy from tasting the *arege* of her customers. When about three-quarters had been bought, she was drunk. At that moment, one of her former lovers arrived in the company of three of his friends. She at first offered them one glass of her *arege*, for free. When they finished that she filled up a Cinzano bottle and handed it over to them. By that time she had decided that she was not going to sell any more of her *arege*, so she sent away anybody who attempted to buy it.

The moment her former lover and his three companions were through with the Cinzano bottle of *arege*, Alicinora lifted what was still left in the jerrycan and, crawling on her knees, placed it in front of the men, giggling like a dimwit. 'Drink it,' she told them. 'Happiness comes from a full stomach.' Then she struck up a beer song:

Lon awoto iwor	He who prowls at night
Lon awoto iwor	He who prowls at night
Mano akwo ġweno	That's a chicken thief
Yelo waa.	He disturbs us.
Lon awoto iwor	He that prowls at night
Lon awoto iwor	He that prowls at night

21

| *Mano akwo gweno* | That's a chicken thief |
| *Kwalo waa.* | He robs us. |

Omako cinge	They grabbed his arms
Ote dwokko ingeye	Twisted them behind him
Ote kob-bi, allo we	They told him: 'You fellow,
Gamente ogik.	your reign is over.'

Then, dropping the first song, she launched into the tail end of another:

Inyomo meri ararac	You marry an ugly woman
Inyomo meri ararac	You marry an ugly woman
Ite moro wangi	Then you rivet
Ikom meg ajoo.	Your lustful eyes
	On other men's wives.

When darkness descended on Loro market, Alicinora was still there, drinking with her male friends and singing at the top of her lungs. She was now dancing too, prancing around on the balls of her naked feet and throwing her arms about like one possessed by the spirit of a soldier shot dead in battle. Those who left the market earlier could still hear her singing clearly in the cold night.

Alicinora left Loro market at the first cockcrow. As she staggered along, following a path that she thought led to her home, she carried her twenty-litre jerrycan, now empty, in her hand. She had stashed away the proceeds from her *arege* in the sash of her old gaberdine *gomesi*. The sash was made by bringing two edges of a strip of cloth together and stitching them closed so that there was space for storing money and other valuables between the two thicknesses of cloth. She had forgotten everything else that she had used for selling her *arege* at the market – glasses, tumblers, plastic cups, bottles and a plastic funnel. She had piled them into her new palm-leaf basket and simply walked away from them. She was too far gone to be aware of her loss.

When sleep overcame her, Alicinora did not know where she was, nor did she care.

It was the early-morning chill that woke Alicinora up. When she awoke she realised that she was lying on the dew-covered verge of a path running through Atengtyena swamp. She sat up, yawned, rubbed her eyes. Where am I? she wondered. Am I really home? Why is it so cold then? Then she looked at the grey expanse of morning sky. And she realised with shock that she had slept out in the cold. She swept her eyes around her. She spotted her yellow jerrycan. It was lying on its side about a metre away to her left. She stretched out her arm, pulled it to herself. Then she supported herself on it to get up. Her *gomesi* fell away from her body. Panicking, she felt around her waist. There was nothing around her waist – the sash-purse had vanished. Somebody has stolen all my money, she thought. Let me hope I have not been raped too. She felt her womanhood with her left hand. There was nothing the matter with it. Suddenly Alicinora became very frightened and she raised the alarm. Ulululululu! Ulululululu! Ulululululu! And she fled up the path on the edge of which she had slept. She was holding her plastic jerrycan firmly by the handle, running as best she could. The *gomesi* flapped wetly against her legs. She stopped briefly, drew up the flapping skirt of the *gomesi* and smelt it. It stank of drunken urine. I have pissed on myself, she told herself, I have pissed on myself like a little child.

Alicinora felt too embarrassed to go back to Teboke that day. Instead she went to the home of one of her friends, Berici, located midway between Loro and Teboke. Alicinora found Berici squatting in front of the door of her sleeping hut, washing her face from a small calabash. Berici took one look at Alicinora and thought: Alicinora will never learn. I have lost count of the number of times I have warned her against heavy drinking. Now she is bringing me more of her troubles, and her shame. Just look at her! She looks like something a sick cow half-chewed and spat out.

Alicinora returned to Teboke the following day, a Sunday, washed and clean, and looking subdued and sober, and very broke. And she was carrying the yellow twenty-litre jerrycan, scrubbed clean as herself, on her sober head.

When this incident had occurred, Olwit had been thirteen and in Primary Seven.

23

But this time around, Olwit was fifteen and in Senior Two. And he was a very angry fifteen. Angry because he wondered why he should be one of the few students in Amuka College who were frequently sent home for non-payment of fees, or for failure to pay part of the fees. Angry because, unlike most of the other children, he could not boast about either of his parents. Musa Wangolo he had only heard about, and nobody seemed to be sure whether he was his real father. In any case, people did not seem to have a very high opinion of him. From what he had heard about him, Musa Wangolo had worked shifts at the ginnery, and to supplement his earnings had fetched water for the Arab shopkeepers when he was on night shift. Musa Wangolo had got fed up with that kind of life when he, Olwit, was still a little child and had wandered away from Teboke, first settling at Aduku where he had become a latrine digger, and then drifting further south to Nambieso, from where he had vanished after about two years. Some people said that Musa Wangolo had crossed Lake Kyoga and taken advantage of his Muslim faith to manoeuvre his way into General Idi's army at Nakasongola. Others insisted that he had gone on digging latrines and had been killed when the walls of a latrine he was digging had collapsed on him. Yet others asserted that it had become increasingly difficult for Musa Wangolo to pay graduated tax and he had eventually fled to one of the floating islands on Lake Kyoga, where he had taken refuge from the sharp-eyed tax collectors. Whatever had been Wangolo's fate, even if it was Wangolo's blood that ran in his veins, he had not been much of a father, for he had never lived with his mother, Olwit had established.

Abudu Olwit was angry because, unlike most of the Senior Two students, his body was a stranger to the feel of trousers and leather shoes, and he did not own a foam mattress. He had to wear shorts all the time. The only footwear that graced his feet were bathroom slippers and car-tyre sandals. He slept on a cotton-filled mattress, the least prestigious kind of mattress to sleep on. His more fortunate school mates called such a mattress *apipi*, stained and worthless cotton residue. Olwit was tired of sleeping on *apipi*, completely, thoroughly fed up.

24

Abudu Olwit was angry because he did not have a religion. He had not been taken to a Muslim *mwalimu* or a Christian priest for religious instruction. He carried a Muslim name, but was not even circumcised. He would have loved to be a Catholic, for his admiration for Fr Guglielmo Varasco, the young ginger-haired Italian priest, was deep. But he was not even baptised. And at fifteen, and being in secondary school, he should at most have been waiting for confirmation, not mere baptism.

So Olwit was very angry indeed that Friday when he arrived home after the duty master, Mr Kula, had called him out of Senior Two Green and told him to either pay up or go home. Only to find a man lying on his mother's belly and grunting like a pig, the door to his mother's sleeping hut not even locked but even a little ajar so that all he had to do was push it and go in and find them at it. Not even waiting for night to fall but doing it in broad daylight with sunheat beating up out of the ground outside his mother's hut and they at it inside, sweating it out in the cool inside of the hut. His head hot, and he dazed by the heat outside and his stomach aching with the hunger of morning and past-midday, and he hoping that his mother would have something for him to eat even if it was only salted pumpkin-leaf soup without groundnut paste, a sweet potato or two, or a few pieces of boiled cassava – at least something to drop into his empty stomach. Only to find them at it, at it without a bit of shame, with the sun barely starting to travel west, the sun so hot and intense outside. And... and Olwit stood hungry and transfixed there at the edge of the bed gazing down at this man whom he had not even seen before, neither at the local market nor anywhere else, this man in the then dark interior of the hut now made light, light pouring in through the wide-open door, and they not even aware of him. Neither this strange man that he was seeing for the first time nor his mother lying there with her eyes turned away towards the circular mud wall of the hut that was dark inside a few moments before but was now light. And he, Olwit, moving zombie-like slightly away from them locked in their enraptured trance, moving away and getting hold of the little *nget* hoe used for weeding millet and simsim and digging up cassava tubers and that his mother used for propping the door of the sleeping hut shut. And he picking up the *nget* lying there beside

25

the door fashioned out of borassus-palm trunk, and moving back to the bed, ever so slowly...And the *nget* going up in his hands and coming down, and up and down, and the inside of the room erupting into utter confusion amidst shrieks and grunts and bewildered pleas. Tangled bodies, two and then three, and blood squirting from one body and dripping from all three... And punches and kicks and shouts and grunts and screams of agony... And flight out into the torrid sun and into the neighbouring sweet patato garden and on to the sorghum field. And Olwit giving chase, the strange man gushing blood and tumbling through the gardens but taking such long and high strides he simply could not be caught...

Chapter III

Fr Guglielmo Varasco had turned up in Teboke when he was least expected. It was rumoured that he had been a lieutenant in the Italian army before taking his holy orders. Short, stout, impulsive and cold-eyed, Fr Varasco relished using his fist to make people see the volcanic power of the Catholic God. When the locals looked at Fr Varasco's flat feet, broad chest, large brow and rust-coloured hair, they sometimes wondered why the thirty-something Italian had been visited upon them.

At the time Fr Varasco first arrived, Teboke was merely a sub-parish attached to Apicil mission, one of the first Catholic missions to be set up in Lango. Its founder, Fr Vittorino Corti of the Verona Fathers, was later to become the second bishop of Lango-Acholi diocese, to which Teboke belonged.

Teboke sub-parish was run by a catechist, Dempterio Arim, a Standard Four dropout. Catechist Arim, a gangling, small-toothed young man with very red gums, had learnt in his few years as a catechist that it was prestigious to act foreign in one's own tribeland. So in his spare time, catechist Arim practised speaking his mother tongue, Lango, with an Italian accent. When he went into the chapel attached to Teboke Elementary School to preach, people sometimes turned up in fairly large numbers to listen to this tall young man with the little, maize-like teeth and very red gums whose mastery of Italian seemed to have so thoroughly spoilt his Lango – even before he had set foot in Italy itself. The Italians at Apicil mission should be very impressed with him, they thought.

Dempterio Arim was very proud of his profession. Once every three days he assembled, instructed and dismissed his curious and admiring catechumens with the aplomb and efficiency of a first-class political cadre. He led the catechumens through the catechism with speed and gusto:

Cakaramento gin adi?   The sacraments, how many are
                         they?

27

Cakaramento gin abiro:	The sacraments, they are seven:
Baticimo	Baptism
Compirimancio	Confirmation
Yugaricitia	The Eucharist
Penitencia	Penitence
Wir maleng	Clean oiling
Orodini	Ordination
Matrimonio!	Matrimony!

Catechist Arim would race through the "counting of the sacraments" as well as other bits of the catechism, his face aglow with pride and triumph. His arms swinging up and down, beating time to the rhythm of his deep catechistic voice. And his knees bending and straightening up in perfect synchronisation.

On first arriving in Teboke, Fr Guglielmo Varasco found a congregation already in place. It had become standard practice to herd all the non-Muslim pupils of Teboke Elementary School – Catholics, Protestants, other non-Christians, non-believers alike – into the chapel attached to the school every Friday so that they could pray, repent of their little sinful ways and look clean in the eyes of the Lord. And their intercessor, catechist Dempterio Arim, would be draped in a white gown behind the simple concrete altar, intoning the prayers in Lango spiked with his rich Italian accent. The adults too, on their part, since the fall of president Bwete and the incipient depredations of the new owner of national power, Idi, had begun to seek solace in chapel-bound worship, especially on Sundays.

The first thing that Fr Guglielmo Varasco did was to stake out land for his mission. No-one was sure whether Fr Varasco had obtained a lease from the National Land Board or not. What Teboke folks noticed one day was that part of Teboke land had started its progress towards becoming mission land.

First the land was marked out.

Then it was fenced with barbed wire.

After that a gate was put in.

Finally concrete likenesses of the Virgin Mary and Jesus were mounted upon the gateposts.

Those whose land had been swallowed up by the mission grumbled loudly but did not take any action.

Except one man. And that man was Laban Oculi. When the newly-acquired mission land was being staked out, Laban Oculi was away in Alito, several miles away from Teboke, visiting relatives. When he returned to Teboke and heard that the mission had taken some of his land, he decided that he was too hot-blooded to take the loss of his land lying down. So one cool evening he hobbled up to the mission to take a look. Indeed his land had been taken – about half an acre.

He looked at the barbed wire fence. He was not much impressed. Nor was he impressed by the concrete statues of Holy Mary and Jesus Christ. Just as talk about the crunching power of Fr Varasco's hard Italian fist had not made much of an impression on him.

As Laban Oculi hobbled away that cool evening, he swore that the next morning he would bring his long-handled Lango hoe to the mission and cultivate the half-acre of his land that had been grabbed. And see if anybody would dare touch him.

Now fifty, Laban Oculi was a leper who had seen military action at the height of his physical prowess. To show that he still felt good despite his leprosy, he would march stiffly through Teboke trading centre shouting:

Lep'...lep'!	Left... left!
Lep'... lep'!	Left... left!
Lep'- rwaiii!	Left – right!
Lep' – rwaiii!	Left – right!
Lep' – rwac!	Left – right!
Lep' – rwac!	Left – right!
Lep' – lep'!	Left... left!
Lep' - lep'!	Left... left!

He would also frequently belt out the Kiswahili song he had sung as a young man in praise of King George of England:

King Jojji
Na mpa salaama

29

Keya
Olee olee olee oleee!

As a young soldier, Laban Oculi had been strong enough to survive the snake-infested jungles of Burma. He had also survived the maddening heat of Misri days and bone-freezing chill of Misri nights.

As a recruit of the King's African Rifles, *kea*, Oculi claimed, he had been injected with a full pint of lion's urine to make him wild and strong, and utterly fearless. This was at a transit camp in Nakuru, Kenya. Laban Oculi, along with other recruits, had been on his way to the Kenyan coast to board the biggest ship that the British had ever built. It was big enough to carry away the entire population of a large county and had two large fields on which they spent their free time playing soccer.

Laban Oculi's British-built ship had cut through many dangerous waves and, after months of chugging and puffing and yawing, had deposited him and his comrandes on the shores of Burma.

In Burma Oculi had fought with valour and beast-like ferocity and put paid to many a Japanese life. The reason why he had been promoted to the prestigious rank of corporal and posted to Misri to fight alongside the great Montgomery, who was then already a famous and feared general. In Misri, too, Oculi had made short work of many enemy, mostly Italians and Germans this time. For this feat he had been rewarded with many colourful medals, which he kept lovingly stored in his tin suitcase built out of cooking-oil *debes*. To show the world that he had performed great feats in the second world-wide war, Oculi had had tattoos done on his left upper arm, fully twenty-four of them, each one, he claimed, standing for a Japanese, Italian or German life he had taken. He had massacred them like flies, Oculi liked to brag.

Laban Oculi took great pride in his intelligence. Look, he never ever forgot whatever *pachwett* his white officers taught him and his comrades, however difficult it was. That was one reason why people like *Leptenan* Williamchon and *Kapten* Ambili would always remember him, even in their England. He never ever forgot *pachwett*.

On his return home from the war, besides his *kea* uniform, Oculi owned two sets of twill shirts and trousers, in addition to two pairs of

30

stout, shiny-black shoes with hard, layered heels and large, square toes. He would frequently don the twills and a pair of the black shoes and swagger around Teboke, brass-knobbed cane in hand and tobacco pipe clamped in mouth.

Smartly dressed as he usually was, he was wont to fight anybody at the slightest provocation. It seemed the pint of lion's urine had not quite left his blood yet. It also seemed that the cruel Misri sun had visited his brain and lodged itself firmly in there.

At that time, whenever Oculi was drunk he would march up the main street of Teboke trading centre shouting, in *kea* English:

> Demful, blanifakin!
> I am like lion!
> I don' care anyone
> I s'oot you one bullet
> An' your head it scatter
> Like calabas'
> I am go Barma
> I am go Michiri
> I am kill Japan
> I am kill Italy
> I am kill Jaman
> I don' care anyone
> I am fight wit' Itila
> I am fight wit' Mucholini
> I am fight wit' Iroyito
> Demful, blanifakin!
> I DON' CARE ANYONE!

Oculi's skin was still smooth and healthy then, unblemished by leprosy. It was generally believed that the leprosy Oculi developed later had been sown on him by one of the many people he had beaten in Teboke after being demobbed from the King's African Rifles.

It has already been mentioned that when Teboke Catholic mission took over Oculi's half-acre of land, he was away in Alito, visiting.

31

A week after Oculi's return from Alito, Fr Guglielmo Varasco found Oculi digging a portion of the land he had secured for his church with a long-handled Lango hoe. He was holding the handle of the hoe with the stumps of his leprosy-severed fingers and shoving the newly-sharpened blade at the shallow roots of the *ototo* plants that thickly covered the ground. Fr Varasco was taking his customary early-morning stroll through the mission grounds when he spotted Oculi. He ambled confidently over to where Oculi was labouring. Oculi pretended complete unawareness of the priest's presence and went on with his digging. The priest got nearer and placed himself directly in Oculi's line of vision, with his arms akimbo. Oculi did not look up but went on digging. He watched Oculi dig for some time in silence . Then he spoke.

'*Dano man,*' he barked, in bad Lango, '*yin itimo ango kan?*' (This person, what do you do here?) He had been taught the basics of Lango at the headquarters of his religious order in Kampala for six months. He spoke the language with a stronger, more genuine Italian accent than Dempterio Arim the catechist did.

Laban Oculi favoured the priest with a look pregnant with contempt and daring. '*An dang atamo ni atem puru potta ni do!*' he replied. (I thought I might as well try to cultivate this garden of mine!)

The priest was quite taken aback by the audacity of the leper's reply.

'This garden of yours? Since when did you have a garden here?' the priest asked.

Laban Oculi stuck the tip of the hoe-blade into the black loam and leaned its handle on the bare leprosy-peeled skin of his right shoulder.

'*Padi,*' he responded. *Padi* is the Lango word for the Italian *Padre*. '*Padi* Guglielmo, I started owning this land long before the Catholics called you to come from Italy and cause trouble for us. I inherited the land from my own father, Opio-Adok. *Padi*, does your father not have enough land there in Italy that you should come here instead and grab our land?'

The priest's cold eyes narrowed to fat-lidded slits.

32

'This person,' he addressed Oculi again, 'I hope you can see this fence. The fence means that the whole of this land belongs to the mission.' Fr Varasco spread his arms wide to embrace the entire expanse of his church's newly acquired land. 'So I am asking you to lift up your hoe and go dig elsewhere .'

'*Padi,*' Oculi said, taking hold of the hoe-handle with both his hands, 'this happens to be my land. Before you took it, you did not ask me whether I wanted to give it away or not. Is it because I am a Protestant that you chose to steal my land?'

'This person,' the priest responded, 'can you understand what I am saying? I am asking you to get out of here now. Right now. Without delay. *Presto*, you hear me?'

Laban Oculi emitted a cold, squawky, mirthless laugh. With the hoe-handle, tightly held, still leaning on his right shoulder. And the newly-sharpened hoe-blade still stuck in the dark loam soil.

'Now, *Padi*,' Oculi said, his mouth twisted in a sinister smile, 'suppose I refused to leave, what would you do? Lift me bodily and throw me over the fence?'

Fr Varasco's ears turned scarlet. His fists clenched. He looked the leper up. He looked him down.

Watery eyes.

Disfigured nose.

Twisted mouth.

Stumpy fingers.

Patches of skin turned pink by disease.

Missing toes – festering sores where they should have been.

And the fetid smell of disease and days-old sweat issuing from his black-and-pink body in nauseous waves.

'Well,' the priest announced, 'I will not cast you out myself. But I will bring somebody who is really good at the job. And when he is through with you, you will wonder what brought you here in the first place.'

'I will be waiting for you right here,' Oculi threatened.

Fr Varasco turned and stalked away in a flurry of brown-sandalled feet and grey trouser-legs. With his arms swinging stiffly at his sides.

Laban Oculi resumed his digging.

A few minutes later the priest returned with the mission *askari*.

The *askari* was carrying a club.

Tall, strapping, snub-nosed and bald-headed, Dominic Lado had fled Sudan during the first round of fighting between northern and southern Sudan. Lado had been a little boy then and had fled with his parents. They had been settled by the United Nations High Commissioner for Refugees in a refugee camp at Adjumani in north-western Uganda. As he grew older, Lado gradually became tired of relying on handouts from the international agency and his parents'control over his life. He wanted to strike out on his own. To earn his own living. To become his own master. So Lado drifted away from the refugee camp, moving southwards and first settling at Atiak, and then moving further south to Gulu town. It was in Gulu that he heard about the cotton ginnery that the Indians had set up in Teboke. So he walked the seventy-odd miles from Gulu to Teboke to see if he could get a job at the ginnery. Surely enough he got one. Loading bales of cotton onto trucks. And offloading them.

Dominic Lado did not like his job. The strength-sapping daily exertion. The contempt and arrogance with which he was treated by both his Indian and African bosses. The callous exploitation. He hated it all.

Dominic Lado was a regular churchgoer, and despite the situation of despair in which he found himself, he did not indulge much in drink. And he was friends with Dempterio Arim the catechist. When Fr Varasco was looking for an *askari* for the mission, therefore, Dempterio Arim had right away thought of Dominic Lado. When Arim had contacted Lado, Lado had agreed to take up the job. The pay was not anything to be excited about, but at least he was given free meals and treated with greater respect and dignity than when he was working at the ginnery.

During the four years he had worked at the ginnery Lado had got to know a number of Teboke folk. He had also developed varicose veins in his right leg.

Lado and the priest approached Oculi, with the priest in the lead, and still scarlet-eared. When they reached within a few feet of Oculi, the priest pointed at him and said, 'That is the man. Throw him out of here.'

Lado knew Laban Oculi. So he addressed him by name.

'Laban,' he said, 'the priest is not happy with you.'

'I know,' Oculi answered, gruffly.

'Now, he wants you to leave. Why don't you want to leave?'

'Dominic,' Oculi responded, 'it is the *padi* who should be asking me why I do not want to leave since he is the one who grabbed my land. Not you.'

The priest was getting impatient. He had brought the *askari* here to cast the intrepid leper out of the bounds of the mission, not to plead with him.

'*Askari,*' the priest said, 'what are you still waiting for? I asked you to throw that man out of here, and all you are doing is chatting.'

What bad luck, Lado thought. He had worked here for barely two weeks and here he was being ordered to place his hands on the diseased skin of a leper. He looked at the priest. Then he looked back at Oculi. He got to within one metre of Oculi, transferred the club to his left hand and held out his right hand. 'Give me that hoe,' he ordered.

Oculi worked up some spittle and spat. Lado jerked his head to the left and jumped back. The leprous spittle landed squarely on Lado's right cheek. His free hand jerked towards his right cheek. Then it jerked away before it had reached the cheek. He was not going to touch a leper's sick spittle with his bare hand. He bent down, yanked free a handful of leaves and wiped the spittle away with them.

'Oculi,' Lado hissed, 'what has got into your head this morning?' A tic was beginning to convulse the spot where Oculi's saliva had landed. 'Why did you spit on my face?'

Oculi gave a brief, raucous, twisted-mouthed laugh. 'It serves you right,' he said. 'Why are you helping the Italian to chase me away from my land? Is that what you came all the way from Sudan for?'

Lado's eyes narrowed to red-eyed slits as his face spasmed even more violently. 'All right,' he said, 'I am off right now. But I will be back shortly, Oculi. And if I find you still loitering around here...' He did not finish the sentence. He wheeled round and stomped away.

35

Fr Varasco stayed behind and glared at Oculi. Oculi glared back. He did not resume digging. He instead leaned the long hoe-handle on his left shoulder.

'*Padi*,' Oculi called out to the priest.

'Do not talk to me,' the priest retorted . 'Wait and talk to Dominic when he comes back.'

Oculi barked out a laugh and muttered while shaking his head: '*Padi...Padi...Padi...Padi...*'

Soon Dominic Lado reappeared. He was fondling a long pink *opobo* whip. Oculi noticed him but did not seem to be particularly concerned.

Lado marched up to Fr Varasco and stationed himself beside him. He swung the whip in an arc. First from left to right. Then from right to left. Then he got hold of its tip and bent it into a bow. And he grinned.

'Oculi,' he said, 'you spat your sick spittle on me as if I had done you a wrong. No-one ever dared spit at me before. Unless you leave right now, today I will give you the kind of lashing that you will remember for the rest of your life!' Then he brought the tip of the whip down hard on the ground and let it rest there. 'Oculi,' he announced, 'I am giving you the last warning. If you do not want to return to your wife with your skin all peeled off, you had better crawl out through the mission fence and go back to her right now. And I repeat, this is the last warning.'

'You can go tell that to your mother!' Oculi spat. Lado's eyes flashed. Lado leapt forward. Two long, brawny, high leaps. And lashed out at Oculi. The *opobo* whip swished and cut at him. At his right arm. His hands came off the hoe and it slid off his shoulders. The whip slashed at the left side of his face. He stifled a cry.

Oculi took awkward-footed steps towards Lado with his arms raised to try and ward off the blows from the whip. Lado swung the whip at his arms. Hard. The arms fell away. Oculi turned and stumbled towards his hoe, in the process turning his back to Lado and the priest. Lado followed him, whipping him on the back. Reaching the spot where the hoe lay, Oculi bent over in an attempt to pick it up. Patches of buttock-skin showed black and glossy

36

through the two large holes in the seat of Oculi's ash-gray, dirt-smeared trousers.

Lado struck the buttocks. The leper's left hand flew to his buttocks as the right hand scrabbled on the ground for the hoe. Fr Varasco exploded in laughter. Haw! Haw! Haw! Haw! Hoo! Hoo! Hoo! Hoo! By the time Oculi straightened up, the priest's eyes were streaming with tears and his body was convulsed with mirth.

After Oculi had straightened up Lado lashed at him one more time. Oculi swung round, hoe in hand, and came face-to-face with his tormentor. He raised the hoe with both hands and aimed its blade at Lado. Lado saw the murderous light in Oculi's eyes and leapt back.

Oculi flung the hoe at him.

Lado tried to twist away from the path of the hoe but failed. The hoe hit him around the hip. He grunted. Dropped the whip. Doubled over. Then he crumpled onto the ground, his hands gripping his right hip.

Oculi stumbled over to where Lado lay writhing. He picked up his hoe and raised it high over the prostrate body.

Fr Varasco shrieked 'Ooh! Ooh! Ooh' as he rushed towards Oculi. Oculi pointed the hoe-blade at Fr Varasco. Lado still lay on the ground, writhing and groaning.

Oculi spoke. '*Padi,*' he said, 'if you do not want to return to Italy wrapped in a mat, do not get near me. Because I will cut you to pieces and then kill your slave Lado too. After all, being a leper, I am already as good as dead. So I do not care. Do you hear me, *Padi*?'

Lado groaned.

The priest pointed at where Lado lay. 'You have hurt him,' he said.

'If he had not thrashed me, I would not have harmed him,' Oculi responded.

'You will pay for this,' the priest threatened.

'Let us wait and see,' the leper answered, unconcerned.

'I am saying that you will be punished for this.'

'I do not care. After all I have already lost my land.'

Fr Varasco did not reply.

Lado groaned.

Oculi lifted his hoe onto his right shoulder and spoke. '*Padi*,' he said, ' I am going now. I am leaving you with your patient.'

The priest's cold eyes flashed. He took one step towards Oculi, then one step back.

Lado groaned.

Oculi smirked and turned away from Fr Varasco.

Fr Varasco walked over to where Lado lay and bent over him. 'Lado...Lado...,' he called.

Lado writhed and groaned.

Oculi limped away towards the mission fence. He pushed down the bottom strand of barbed wire with his hoe and stepped out.

***

Two days later Oculi was arrested and taken to Atura Police Station. At the station he was told that he would be charged with trespass and causing grievous bodily harm. 'I do not care,' he responded.

Dominic Lado did not die.

Chapter IV

Three years after Fr Guglielmo Varasco's arrival. Teboke Catholic mission was firmly rooted now. Fr Varasco's sharp tongue, I-don't-give-a-damn attittude and abrasive energy had won him lots of enemies. And also lots of friends. Within the three years Fr Varasco had set up a large mission house, an old people's home and a borehole pump. He had also planted a stand of eucalyptus trees and established an orange orchard. Furthermore, he had purchased four oxen which those catechumens residing in the mission used for ploughing the mission land. Fr Varasco had promised his parishioners a Fiat tractor in the very near future.

Many of the people who came into contact with Fr Varasco loved, hated, feared and were awed by him in equal measure. The priest did not seem particularly concerned about what people thought or said about him. He seemed too completely bent on developing the mission to mind : he was too busy setting up one project after another. He also seemed completely focused on converting as many people as possible to the Catholic faith.

When they met for the first time, the Honourable Mike Adoli-Awal and Fr Guglielmo Varasco at once took a strong liking to each other. When Bwete's first government fell, therefore, Adoli-Awal and the priest had become fast friends.

***

Bwete's first fall had taken Adoli-Awal completely by surprise...

Feet thudding on hard ground. Hands thumping breast, frantic. Worry piped into gabled *mabati* house, voice hoarse and thin with fright and world-end worry. Whispered concern shrilled into Adoli-Awal's house through crack between doorjamb and door of sitting-room.

'Adoli! Adoli! *Bwete be dong pe!*' (Adoli! Adoli! Bwete is no more!)

January twenty-fifth. Bwete had fallen. Fallen unpresent in his own country but making deep and important noises in a faraway land. Noises about things that were perhaps important, perhaps not.

The children had expected the grass to turn blue. Or any grass-unfamiliar colour. For Bwete meant president. Nay PRESIDENT. P-R-E-S-I-D-E-N-T. In capital letters. *ADWONG LOBO*: the owner of the land, of Uganda. Bwete was the PRESIDENCY. He and the presidency were two parts of authority welded into an invincible symbiosis. Annealed. Unbreakable. Immune to fracture or fissure. Even under the heavy sledge hammer of a brutal military coup.

The children had expected the grass to turn blue. Or another grass-unfamiliar colour. For had it not been said that Bwete lived underground under the tight and watchful guard of soldiers so totally dedicated and committed to his safety that they could for days dispense with the affectionate arms of their wives, their cushiony bellies? Was Bwete not always bunkered in underground invincibility, in amniotic security deep inside the womb of his presidential sanctum? So safe even flies and mosquitoes would get lost in the labyrinth of concrete tunnels that led to his abode?

The children had expected the grass to turn blue. Or any other grass-unfamiliar colour.

But the grass did not turn blue. The grass stayed green that year, the year after, and during all the years that followed.

'Adoli! Adoli! *Bwete be dong pe! En akobbi ni!*'(Adoli! Adoli! Bwete is no more! I am telling you!)

Frantic fist-rap on door of living-room. Door of strong mahogany wood. But fist sufficiently fear-strong to strike a clear message through wood and intervening space to reach Adoli-Awal and family settled around a pot of millet beer, sucking warm contentment into their beer-accustomed bellies.

'There seems to be bad trouble,' Adoli-Awal tells his family. 'Let me go and check.'

He goes to the strong mahogany door and opens it a little. 'Who is it?' he asks, his voice gruff, impatient.

'It is me, Rucita.'

Adoli-Awal knows Rucita. It must be *the* Rucita. So he opens the door wider so that she can get through. Inside the living-room Rucita tells them about what she has heard on the radio. In the heat of the dry-season day. On that selfsame twenty-fifth day of January.

40

Bwete had fallen. And the new *Adwong Lobo*, master and owner of Uganda, was *the* Idi.

Adoli-Awal tells Rucita that he, too, has heard about the fall of Bwete. Also in the heat of the day. On his car radio. The radio in the long, black Benz with the silver trim. On his way back to the capital, Kampala. He had found the news alarming. So he had turned his big, black Benz around and come back home to Teboke. And now here he was drinking millet beer with his family. And trying to think things through.

***

Mike Adoli-Awal had become a member of parliament a few months before the British placed real power in the hands of Uganda's blacks. And Adoli-Awal had retained his parliamentary seat until president Bwete had made his ill-fated Commonwealth trip to Singapore and lost his job to Major General Idi. This was slightly more than ten years after Adoli-Awal had first been elected to parliament. Suddenly the House of Parliament, within whose precincts he had debated deep and serious issues, had become a very dangerous place indeed. The result was that Adoli-Awal suddenly found himself devoid of a seat in parliament and therefore out of a job. And being a card-carrying member of the Party of the Palm like the now exiled Bwete, it would not have been wise for him to seek out Major General Idi and ask him for a job. Too many of his friends and former colleagues had begun to disappear from their homes and workplaces and end up dead in forests or inside the bellies of fish and crocodiles. Frequently with their heads or genitals or both missing.

Despite all that was happening and all that he was hearing about the nature of Major General Idi's rule, Adoli-Awal stayed put in his village. In hiding. Venturing out only occasionally to visit friends and relatives, often at night. And sometimes on a Sunday going to one out-of-the-way Catholic chapel or other to attend service, but never going to the same chapel two or three times in a row.

Two things eventually decided Adoli-Awal against staying on in Uganda.

The first was a rumour that engulfed Teboke that a boy from Lwala, one of the neighbouring villages, had become an Army

41

Intelligence informant and had been heard asking about him one Friday at Loro market.

The second was an event that shocked a lot of people. A middle-aged man had gone to Okole swamp to fish but instead of spearing a fish, he had speared a human head. The man in question was called Leben Odul.

Leben Odul was known in Teboke and all the neighbouring villages for his fishing skills—whether with a fish hook or a fish spear. The day Odul speared the human head he had gone to Okole swamp earlier than usual in a group of ten people. It was December. The dry-season heat had drunk up the water so that the swamp, which normally ate up a tall man's height, now only swallowed such a man up to the waist.

Two days earlier Odul had been very lucky. He had gone back home with a big lungfish, a fat, egg-filled catfish and a green-shelled water tortoise. Though she disapproved of his eating tortoises, his wife, Rojo, had welcomed him back with a warm bath and a pot of millet beer. Then she had prepared for him a supper of smoked goat in groundnut-paste soup and mashed cassava.

But that was two days ago.

Today on his way to Okole swamp Leben Odul had struck a stone with his left big toe. He knew that this was supposed to portend bad luck but it had happened to him before and no ill-luck had befallen him. Still he walked towards Okole swamp with a heavy heart.

The human head was the first thing he speared. When his spear struck the human head he thought it was that of a catfish since catfish had very hard heads. Or the shell of a water tortoise. So he leaned the whole of his weight on the shaft of his spear. And belted out the praise chant of his mother's clan:

Oluku yoo!	She has come back!
Oluku yoo!	She has come back!
Wong-wong idwongo!	Her basket on her head!
Wong-wong idwongo!	Her basket on her head!
Yam ikobo ni Odul mom puru!	Yet she had claimed that
	Odul was too lazy to dig!

42

Yam ikobo ni Odul mom puru!	She had claimed that Odul was too lazy to dig!
Aco Odul bade tek!	Yet Odul's arm is strong!
Bad Odul tek!	Odul's arm is strong!
Aman tye anekko rec!	Now Odul is killing fish!
Anekko rec apita!	Killing fish In their hundreds!

Yet even as he belted out the praise-chant, Odul was not quite sure that he should be chanting. His heart beat the wrong way. It was not the racy thudding of excitement. Instead it was the heavy, irregular lurch of apprehension. What was this accursed thing that suffered the thrust of a spear without thrashing around? Was it anything live? Any living thing would have been violently thrashing around in an attempt to set itself free. But this thing lay utterly calm and unbothered. Limp. Like an impotent man's worthless organ.

Odul turned to his neighbour to the left, his face creased with worry.

'Apali,' he called. Apali was furiously thrusting away with his spear. 'Apali,' Odul said, 'there is something I have speared here. I cannot quite understand its nature.'

'Let me come and see,' Apali said as he waded over to where Odul was. Apali looked at the shaft of Odul's spear for some time. It was not shaking. 'Odul,' Apali said, 'your spear-shaft is not moving. Is your fish really thrashing around?' Apali laughed nervously and spluttered.

'That is what is worrying me,' Odul replied, grim concern in his voice. 'The thing is not moving at all. It seems to be a dead thing.'

Now it happened that Apali was known for his courage. One time, in the same swamp, he had grabbed the neck of a big water snake that had struck a friend, strangled it and cast it onto the murram road cutting through the swamp.

'Now Odul,' Apali said, 'hold the spear-shaft firmly. I shall feel whatever it is you have speared.' And his arm slid down the portion of shaft under the water, groping, checking. Soon his head disappeared under the muddy water.

Suddenly Apali's head shot up into view and Apali fell backwards into the water, his face contorted with fright. As Apali's back struck the water Odul took two water-encumbered steps away from his spear-shaft. Then he stopped dead. One of the other fish hunters asked him, 'Odul, what is the matter?'

Odul pointed at where his spear-shaft stood aslant in the water. 'What Apali's hand touched beneath that spear was not good,' he said. 'He acted like one who had seen a terrible sight.' By now Apali had re-emerged from beneath the swamp water. Everyone in the swamp had stopped to listen.

'Apali, what was it?' Odul asked.

'I do not know,' Apali replied, thoughtfully. 'I do not know. It was round. And had hair all around it. Coarse hair. Odul, it is difficult to tell what strange object your spear has impaled, but I do not think it is anything good.'

'Now you all move away,' Odul advised his fellow hunters, who had gathered around him and Apali. 'I will lift it and see what it is.'

Oooop! And a severed human head shot up into the air, impaled on the end of Odul's spear. His fellow hunters shouted, almost in unison: '*Wii dano*!' (A human head!) Then they scrambled away, wading through the water, stumbling, flailing, falling and rising.

Odul dropped the spear and the impaled head and fled.

The next day the local parish chief put together a team to search for the spear-and-head. They found it floating about half a kilometre away from where Odul had speared it. The head was identified right away. It had belonged to Marko Owilli, a trader from Corner Kamdini who had travelled to Malaba on the Uganda-Kenya border a week earlier to buy some goods for his shop. Or he was supposed to have travelled to Malaba. Marko Owilli had been a staunch supporter of the Party of the Palm, the political party led by deposed Bwete, and one of its minor officials. A few months before his death it had been heard that State Security agents had been looking for him.

When Mike Adoli-Awal heard about the head he decided not to set eyes on it. His mind was made up. He was going to leave the country. That very week. If little people such as shopkeepers were getting beheaded, what chances did his own head stand, he who

44

possessed a master's degree and who had been an Honourable Member of Parliament?

Three days after the accidental spearing of Owilli's head Fr Varasco drove Mike Adoli-Awal in his grey Peugeot 404 pick-up through the Uganda-Kenya border and deposited him at a Catholic mission in Eldoret. Adoli-Awal wore a black clerical shirt and white dog collar for the trip. His altered passport told the soldiers at the many roadblocks they encountered that he was Fr Paul Githongo, a Kenyan national working at the Mbuya Catholic mission in Kampala.

Mike Adoli-Awal was to stay in exile in Kenya for six years. He only returned to Uganda after Idi had been removed by armed Ugandan exiles and Tanzanian troops. Adoli-Awal did not take part in the fight to oust Idi, though he made a lot of articulate and intelligent noises in many foreign capitals. This was one of the reasons why he was appointed Managing Director of the National Manufactory of Shoes and Uniforms and awarded many directorships under the second Bwete regime.

***

Before the first fall of President Bwete, Mike Adoli-Awal had known neither hiding – except in play – nor suffering in his life. His father *Rwot* Awal, a county chief, had made sure that his son received the best care that the first-born son of the first wife of a county chief could get. He was a chief, a *rwot*, and his son was no *akopi*, commoner! It was only the sons of commoners who were meant to suffer.

***

Chief Awal had liked confiding in his son, even when he was still a little boy. 'These people here,' he had one time told him, referring to the people he governed, his commoners, 'are stupid. Their heads are rotten with stupidity. My father brought the white man to them and they at first ran away from him. Because the white man wanted them to wear cotton cloth instead of cowskin strips and cowhide genital aprons. They believed that the white man had put disease in his cotton cloth. And when *dokta* Aligijana came with his needle and the liquid herb that cured yaws, they fled and hid in the bushes,

45

thinking that Aligijana wanted to draw all the blood from their bodies. My father had to send his men into the bushes to flush them out like guinea fowl.

'The bicycle that Aligijana gave my father was the first one I rode. Wherever I passed, the commoners stopped by the side of the road and gaped in awe. And whenever a tyre went flat all I had to do was request a goat to be slaughtered so that the tyre could get full again. My request was always granted.' Chief Awal chuckled. 'I told you that their heads are rotten with stupidity. I was clever. That is why the white man chose me to go to King's College Budo in Buganda and learn his knowledge for two years. You too, I want you to go to Budo and acquire the white man's knowledge there. I can already hear the rumblings of anger and impatience among the people of Buganda, even though here we are still quiet. The people of Buganda want the white man to go back to his country. Are you listening, my son?'

'Yes, father.'

'If you are listening that is good. I want you to study hard when you go to school. The white man may not go today or tomorrow. But when he goes I want you to be one of the people who will take his place. And drive a long *Pwoda* car like that of the *pici* in Gulu, or like that of the *gabuna* in Entebbe.'

***

At the age of fifteen, after Mike Adoli-Awal had finished Standard Six, his father had sent him off to a friend, and a former Budo King's College classmate, Petero Lwanga, 'to find him a place in a good junior secondary school.' Petero Lwanga had placed Adoli-Awal in the best junior secondary school in his county, Mugendawala Junior Secondary. And promptly converted him from the Protestant faith to the Catholic.

Unknown to Chief Awal, Petero Lwanga, who had been a Protestant, had fallen out with his Protestant mentors when he had been passed over for a ministerial appointment in the Buganda government. In retaliation he had renounced his Protestant faith and converted to Catholicism. And proceeded to order all members of

46

his vast household to change too, threatening to disown all those who refused.

Chief Awal did not know that his son had become a Catholic until he heard that he had entered Namilyango College. Now it happened that Namilyango, being a Catholic-founded school, and one of the best secondary schools in the country, gave priority to Catholic students. How come his son had found it easier to join a Catholic-founded school than Budo, a Protestant-founded one, though he was a Protestant?

When Chief Awal learnt about his son's conversion, he first travelled to Petero Lwanga's home to quarrel with him, then proceeded to Namilyango. His intention was to withdraw his son from Namilyango College, convert him back to the Protestant faith, and then find him a place in King's College Budo. At Namilyango College, however, he met an implacable headmaster, Fr McCormarck.

Fr McCormarck's nostrils were mere slashes, so that when he spoke the sounds of his speech seemed to catch up in his nostrils before they could squeeze themselves through.

'Mr Awal,' he said, after Chief Awal had explained the reason for his visit, 'since your son is already a student here, I would suppose it would be unreasonable for you to withdraw him now. In any case, he is one of the really brilliant students here, and this school is as good as any other you'll find.'

'With all respect to you, Father,' Chief Awal responded, 'I never contemplated that my son would transform into a Catholic. I humbly beg that my son be allowed to transfer to Budo so that he can follow in my footmarks.'

'I'm sorry, Mr Awal,' Fr McCormarck said, 'right now the students are quite busy in class. Perhaps you could wait for your son to come out for lunch and then talk to him then. In my office. Good morning.' And the good Father offered him his hand.

It was 9 a.m. Chief Awal had driven in his large, black Zephyr car all day the previous day and then spent the night with a friend in Kampala. He had been too angry to sleep that night. When lunch time came and Chief Awal had the opportunity to talk to his son, he was surprised by his son's adamance. 'I am already a Catholic,' his son said, ' in a Catholic school with a lot of Catholic friends. It is a good school, father, and the priests and teachers treat me well. And I am doing well in class. And in sports too. So why do you want to transfer me, father?'

Chief Awal had argued with his son to no avail. Seething with anger, he had told his son never to set foot in his home again until he had become a Protestant once more. Mike Adoli-Awal had obliged him and stayed away for the remaining three years of his Cambridge School Certificate course. Fr McCormarck had taken Mike Adoli-Awal under his wing.

When Chief Awal heard about how well his son had performed in the Cambridge School Certificate exams, he drove all the way to Namilyango College, with Adoli-Awal's mother beside him, to pick him up.

***

Chief Awal had worried that his son's Catholicism might be held against him by the movers and mentors of the Party of the Palm, a predominantly Protestant political party. Or that, because of the vast influence of his family, the Party of the Cock – a predominantly Catholic party – would attempt to lure him in order to fully capitalise on the influence of his family and his education.

What was worrying Chief Awal did not, however, materialise. When Mike Adoli-Awal stood for parliament, he received solid support not only from the most senior Party of the Palm politicians, but also from Bwete himself. As a result he won 65 percent of the vote in his constituency – Ayer – soundly beating his Party of the Cock opponent, Santonino Opio, a fellow Catholic.

Chapter V

*Other women's sons are hot. They sleep with their sweethearts only once and make them pregnant. Many of my agemates already have grandchildren but I have none. I have kept my ears cocked for a long time but I have not yet heard that my son is going after this one's daughter or that one's. And my fellow women laugh at me. They call my son **apele**, a worthless, effeminate apology for a man. What could be wrong with my son? When I gave birth to him I kept him indoors for the first three days as custom demanded. And I respected his delicate waist and scrotum. I never touched them, not even by mistake, not even in my sleep. For I never wanted to damage my son, to make him impotent. Now what bad thing could have happened to him? When he was a little boy and I still had the freedom to watch him naked, he would get up in the morning with his little manhood standing up stiff as a stick. And when he peed his urine would shoot hot and high from here to there. What has happened to my son? Has he perhaps slept with a sorcerer's daughter who has stolen his manhood so that now it cannot function like other women's sons'? Otherwise why does my son not also plant his seeds in people's daughters like other people's sons so that I can stop being a laughing-stock?*

Alicinora had worried a great deal about her son, Abudu Olwit, when he was in secondary school. She was always thinking about the predicament he had put her in, about when he would bring a girl to her home, a girl who, so to speak, would be around to take out millet chaff in case it fell in her eye. Look, he was born seventeen years ago and already in 'senior', yet he did not have a girlfriend. She had done everything, everything a woman could think of. She had encouraged girls to visit him in his hut but all he did was look at them like a dog watching an *otule* dance, with absolute lack of interest. She had deliberately embarrassed him a number of times in the presence of her fellow women and young girls by ordering him to stoke the fire in the kitchen. He had obeyed the first few times and then had refused each time after that. Many times she had shouted after him 'Get me somebody to mend the fire for me!' as he stalked off to his hut or elsewhere, his mien dark as a storm. Look, many of his agemates already had children, some with as many as four girls, yet her son had none, not even just one. What was he still waiting for? *Cede*, she was not going to continue suffering the shame of cooking for a child whose manhood was already hairy. As if she was his girlfriend! She was going to teach him a lesson!

***

It was a Wednesday. Teboke market day. Abudu Olwit could remember it very well. He had got up early as usual and gone off to his cassava garden to weed it before the sun's rays became strong and sharp. He had worked until late morning and then returned home. His mother was nowhere to be seen. He thought that perhaps she was weeding the sweet potato garden behind her sleeping hut, which was locked with a cheap Diamond lock. Alicinora was not in the potato garden. He thought she had gone to the well, so he went back to his round hut and sat down on the banked-up earth that was its verandah. He was feeling very hungry and it was coming to midday, yet his mother was still nowhere to be seen. He went to the three-stone fireplace. He thought that there were perhaps some coals hidden beneath the grey ashes that spilt from within the enclosure formed by the three fire-stones onto the area of floor around the hearth. There was not a single live coal under the ashes. There was no fire in the fireplace. That meant that his mother had not thought of cooking anything for them to eat. He got hungrier still, so he picked up his hoe and went back to the cassava garden. He dug up a big cassava tuber and ate it raw.

***

That Wednesday his mother did not return. When he asked some of those who had been at the market whether they had seen her there, they told him that they had not.

The next day she did not show up either. Anxious and worried, Olwit went to his uncle Odwong's home, five miles away at Alemi

50

trading centre, on the Friday. He intended to find out whether his uncle knew anything about the whereabouts of his mother.

'Your mother came here on Wednesday night. Yesterday I asked her what had brought her here and she said she had only come to tell me that she was tired of cooking for you as if you were still a child, and she was on her way to Agwata to stay with Abuli.'

Abuli was Alicinora's younger sister. Odwong was the eldest child in Alicinora's family. The second child, also a boy, had died of measles at the age of eighteen months. At that time Alicinora's late mother was already seven months pregnant with Alicinora. Abuli came exactly two years after Alicinora's birth. Alicinora's mother then developed strange swellings on her body and her skin peeled off in parts. Her eyes became all red and watery and her mouth twisted to one side. Later some of her toes and fingers rotted away. Her husband's people suspected that one of her enemies had sown leprosy on her body, probably out of envy since, because her womb was sound and she was bearing children so frequently, she seemed destined to fill her husband's compound with children. When his wife's condition had got really bad, Alicinora's father, Erinayo, had abandoned her and gone off to Nambieso on the shores of Lake Kwania, many, many miles away from his village. There he had taken up with a Muruli woman and gone on to make many healthy children with her.

When Odwong had migrated to Alemi from his birthplace at Aloi, Alicinora had come with him as a little girl. A few years later, feeling restless, she had embarked on her own migration – to Teboke. Like Alicinora, Abuli had never married, and kept flitting from place to place like a tadpole.

'My mother humiliates me all the time,' Olwit complained to his uncle. 'Especially when she is selling *arege*. She is always shouting at me in front of other people, even strangers. "Go stoke the fire, it is about to die out!" "Don't you know that it is time to move the goats to where there is better grazing?" "Look how he is dressed! A man like you still cannot button his shirt properly?" All, all the time my mother humiliates me. I wonder what I have done to her to make her treat me like that.'

51

'My son,' Odwong said gently, 'your mother has had problems right from the time she was a girl. I do not think she ever liked children much.' Odwong paused a little. 'Well, now that you are here, you can stay for as long as you like.'

When Odwong told him about the possibility that his mother might not have liked children much, this information dredged up a memory that had long become vague in his head. He would have been around six or seven at that time. In his childhood yearning for nice things to eat he had stolen a little of his mother's money. It had been five shillings, which he had used to buy a cluster of ripe *amemmo* bananas. When his mother had discovered the theft of the five shillings she had caned him heavily with a thin branch that she tore off a thorn tree. Some of the thorns from that branch had embedded themselves in his flesh and had to stay there until pus had formed around them. When the pus had formed, the thorns were squeezed out. That was, however, a long time ago.

Right now, his uncle was inviting him to stay at his home for as long as he liked. Abudu Olwit knew that it was difficult for him to stay for more than a day or two at a time in his uncle's home. One reason was that he had his mother's goats to mind. Right now they had to be hungry and thirsty since he had last taken them out to graze yesterday and they certainly were still tethered to the roof supports of her mother's run-down kitchen. He also had to watch over his mother's and his own meagre belongings in addition to working in the gardens and protecting the crops against invasion by stray goats and sheep from neighbouring homes.

The following morning Abudu Olwit returned to his mother's home.

***

Olwit did not know that Jacinta Apio did not have all her spirit around her until he had lived with her for a week. He was to learn after the one week that part of her spirit had been stolen by *jogi* when she had been abducted by them and kept underground for a number of days.

52

Jogi were small, ugly, stocky man-like creatures that lived either underground in woods and forests or in places where there were large expanses of rock. They invariably had very large heads. Just like humans, they varied in age. They were the spirits of dead people that had taken on human form, yet they were hardly friendly to humans. They quite frequently appeared to humans, especially where there was a large *olam* or *itek* tree, or where there were large numbers of anthills or termite mounds, which they sometimes chose to inhabit. If a *jok* – for that was how one of them was called – or *jogi* appeared to you, you had to hurry home. On arriving home you had to go straight to bed, even if it was still broad daylight. Early the following morning you had to twirl a piece of *moko*– fermented and roasted millet dough from which millet beer is made – around your head and fling it as far away as your arm could send it. The bad luck that the encounter with the *jok* or *jogi* would have brought went away with the piece of *moko*.

Jacinta Apio was the name of the girl with the denuded spirit that Olwit brought home.

One day Jacinta Apio had gone to fetch firewood at Te-Bung in Aduku. She had been all alone. She had built up a large pile of firewood from branches that she had broken off standing trees. Then she had stood the bundle of firewood, now tied with *iponga* bark, up against a large *itek* tree and sat down to rest before she could have enough strength to lever the firewood onto her head and carry it home. A few seconds after sitting down she was overcome by a great, limp-numbing lethargy. Her eyes grew heavy. Her head felt as if it was stuffed with rock. Then she fell asleep.

Only she did not fall asleep. The sensation of sleep marked her transit from the land of *ji* – the living – to the netherworld of the *jogi* – the spirits.

In the twilight of the netherworld, a grandmother spirit came hobbling to Jacinta Apio on her dry, wrinkled limbs with the support of a long gnarled *icac* stick. Her long, thin neck was bedecked with loose strings of cowrie shells that clacked and rattled as she walked. She leaned over Jacinta Apio and gave her a toothless, black-gummed smile. Jacinta was seated on a small earth dais all numb and heavy and unable to move. She felt as if she had been carried and placed there by some power that was stronger than humans.

'Granddaughter,' the grandmother spirit spoke, leaning her frail, withered body over Jacinta. Her left arm rested on her bent waist. 'Granddaughter,' she said again, 'I am very happy that you have visited us. Above-earth people do not visit us often, so when we see one, we are really delighted. Especially if it is a young girl like you.' The elderly spirit paused briefly. 'When you left your home to fetch firewood, how were the above-earth people?'

Jacinta could not reply. She tried though. She wanted to say something in response. But her tongue felt very heavy, unliftable. As if something had been placed on it to keep it firmly down on its floor. And it seemed to have grown larger, to have completely filled her mouth. Yet she was breathing with ease.

The grandmother spirit seemed to have sensed her predicament. She emitted a short, hollow cackle and spoke again. Despite the numbness that suffused her body, Jacinta shivered.

'That is the way it is at the beginning, granddaughter,' the grandmother spirit addressed Jacinta, straightening up. 'You are unable to speak now. But when you become one of us your tongue will be untied. And you will talk as much as the rest of us do – perhaps even more.' She cocked her big, clean-shaven head to one side and squinted at Jacinta.'You are hungry, are you not?' she asked. Then she went on to supply the answer. 'Yes, you are hungry, granddaughter. After all that hard work breaking branches off our trees and stacking them up, you must be very hungry.' She paused a little. 'Well, I am leaving now. But I will send one of your agemates, Adebe, with a meal for you.' And the grandmother spirit turned and hobbled away, her cowries clattering and rattling noisily.

A little while afterwards a young girl spirit appeared from the direction in which the grandmother spirit had disappeared. Just like Jacinta's, Adebe's breasts were still orange-small. Unlike Jacinta who was fully clothed, however, all Adebe wore was a small patch of goatskin over her womanhood and a long, thin strip of goatskin over the cleft between her buttocks. Adebe was carrying a small gourd in her left hand and a large smoke-blackened potsherd in her right. She approached Jacinta and placed the gourd and the potsherd in front of her.

Without preamble, she pointed to the potsherd. 'There is your food,' she said, 'eat it.' Then she pointed at the gourd. 'There is your water,' she said, 'drink it.' Then she went back to wherever she had come from.

Suddenly whatever seemed to have been weighing down on Jacinta seemed to ease off. She felt lighter. She could move her limbs. Her head seemed lighter. She could move her tongue. She thrust her tongue out and licked her lower lip. Then her upper lip. The smell of the food in the potsherd wafted up to her nose. She liked what she smelt. She picked up the gourd. It was dark-brown and old and smelt as if it had been smeared with simsim oil. She turned it around. There was a round hole in its round belly, slightly below the joint between the neck and the belly. So the gourd had been fashioned into an *okoli,* she thought. Where she came from an *okoli* was used strictly to perform traditional rites. Just like the gnarled *icac* stick that the grandmother spirit had used to support herself. Jacinta Apio swished the water in the *okoli* around. Then she tipped some of the water into her right palm and put the *okoli* back on the floor. She washed her hands with the little water. After that she stretched out her legs, leaned over and picked up the potsherd. She looked closely, squinting in the dim light at the contents of the potsherd. There were some brownish, little, nice-smelling things in there. She grabbed up a handful, opened out her palm and looked more closely. It was maggots. She was looking at maggots – lush, fat, roasted maggots. Her fingers went slack. The maggots in her palm slid to the floor. Then she let go of the potsherd. And threw up.

***

Three days later Jacinta's two brothers and her mother found her seated with her back against a large *itek* tree, her bundle of firewood leaning against the tree trunk next to her. She could neither speak nor rise up. Her mother had to carry her back home on her back.

Jacinta's people suspected what could have happened to her. It would not be the first time that the *jogi* had abducted someone.

They had abducted a few young people before, mostly girls. Some had been recovered, others had not. Those who had not returned were the gluttons, for an abductee was always offered a dish of maggots. The moment the abductee so much as tasted the maggots he would not be allowed to return above earth. He would forever live in the netherworld of the spirits.

That Jacinta had returned to the surface meant that she had not eaten the maggots. Her mother was happy and proud. She had taught her daughter well. As a result she had turned out to be the kind of girl who would not go eating anything placed before her. Some of the spirits who abducted her would, however, have entered her before she was returned to the surface. The moment Jacinta arrived back home, her mother thought, she would look for a powerful medicine man to cleanse her of spirit-habitation.

***

On returning home from his uncle's home, Olwit realised that he just had to find somebody to run his mother's abandoned home. The problem was that he did not have a girlfriend. Even if he had one, it would still have been unwise to bring her home, especially if she was a Teboke girl, or if she came from one of the nearby villages. If that was the case, her parents were likely to follow her soon after and cause him a lot of trouble. He decided to wait until the next Teboke market day and pick up a girl who came from far away. He hoped that by the time her parents tracked her down he would have gone back to school and his mother would have to bear the brunt of their anger. And, of course, she would have to pay them the elopement fine, the *luk*.

The next market day Olwit decked himself out in his school uniform, complete with badge and stockings. Amuka College, Olwit's secondary school, was one of the most prestigious secondary schools in the country. Wearing an Amuka College uniform set you above everybody else and conferred upon you a unique and awe-inspiring distinction. Quite frequently uneducated young men would borrow a uniform from an Amuka College student in an attempt to impress their girlfriend or the parents of their intended bride. The more

56

enterprising ones borrowed the uniforms along with the identity cards of the owners, and sometimes to emphasise their sophistication, tucked the tails of the uniform shirts into their brief pants, hitching the waistband of the pants up into full public view. Any modern man worth his salt had to show to the world not only that he was educated, but also that he was sophisticated enough to know the value of multi-coloured factory-made synthetic underwear, and thus wear it instead of the locally made pants contemptuously referred to as *cukuleke.*

That market day, therefore, found Abudu Olwit decked out in his white poplin shirt, khaki shorts and blue stockings with the white bands around their tops. The badge that he proudly carried over his shirt pocket bore the picture of a rhino and beneath the rhino proudly announced: ***RYEKO YA IWORO (WISDOM COMES FROM RESPECT).***

Olwit was very smart, but was very frightened too. The day before, he had sold some cassava to an *arege* brewer. His pocket was therefore not exactly empty. Abudu bought large quantities of drink that day – *arege, acoi* beer and *kwete.* The *arege* he bought mainly for himself – he desperately needed it to obtain alcohol-induced courage. The *kwete* he bought mostly for the girls along with the *kabalagala* pancakes to go with it.

What first drew Olwit's attention to Jacinta Apio, the girl who had been abducted by the spirits, was her smile. Jacinta's smile was soft and mellow, it was mild and bewitching like smouldering simsim pods.

Jacinta had come from Aduku, a place located to the south-east of Teboke, several kilometres away. Her blue-and-white print dress and mauve plastic high-heeled shoes set her squarely apart from the rest of the girls at the market, who mostly wore gaberdine dresses and rubber bathroom slippers.

Abudu Olwit thought that the school uniform he wore and the *kwete* and pancakes he had bought for Jacinta were enough to impress her. So he told her he was interested in her.

'You want me?' she asked, not looking surprised at all. Unlike most of the girls he knew, Jacinta did not look coyly down. Nor did she attempt to avoid his eyes. Instead she looked directly at him. Into his eyes. At his badge. At his khaki shorts. Down to his stockings and black well-shined shoes. Olwit's stomach clenched. Was she going to reject him?

And then Jacinta smiled her soft, smouldering simsim-pod smile. Her smile almost threw him off balance. The gentle beauty of it. Its subtly mocking quality.

'I wanted to take you home,' Olwit said, almost choking on the words, 'so that you can cook for me.'

This time she laughed – very cautiously though, covering her mouth with both her hands and allowing only so much sound to escape.

'I would have thought you would first seek out my parents and tell them that you wanted me to cook for you,' she said.

This girl is mocking me, Olwit worried. Look at the light in her eyes. Is it not the light of deep, unimpressed mockery? 'Jacinta,' he said. He could not believe that the fluttering and churning in his stomach did not register in his voice. Uncertainty. Fright. The fear of rejection, of the girl going off to tell her friends about his failed attempt. Oh the shame and embarrassment of it all! 'Jacinta, people do not meet just once and the man decides right away to see your parents. He must first get to know you.'

'But you already know me,' Jacinta countered. 'If you did not know me, would you be calling me Jacinta?'

Olwit wished he had met a shyer, less obstinate girl, the type who would pluck off a piece of grass and chew it to pulp as she mumbled to him, while all the time staring at the area of ground around her feet.

'Calling you Jacinta does not mean knowing you. It does not mean knowing you properly. It only means knowing your name,' Olwit responded. 'I want to take you home so that I can know you better. So that you can see the inside of my dwelling. So that you can meet my people.'

'Your people?' Jacinta asked and laughed. Her laugh was quiet. It seemed to escape from deep within herself. Secretive. Subtle. Not wanting to be too obtrusive. 'We meet for the first time only today and you already want to show me to your people? What if it turns out I am the daughter of a wizard?'

58

'Your eyes are too white to be those of a wizard's daughter,' Olwit answered. This time she laughed loud. And short. The way mature village women laugh. Eh-hey!

'Do not tell me that the eyes of wizards' daughters are not white! Eh-hey!'

Olwit was sweating. Sweating on his forehead. Sweating in his palms. Sweating on his back. The sweat running down his back into the cleft between his buttocks.

Eh-hey! Jacinta laughed once more. And covered her mouth with both her hands. About wizards' daughters not having white eyes, he had said that partly in jest and partly in seriousness. The eyes of a wizard, and of those of his offspring whom he had infected with his evil powers, were red like those of the pepper-eating *apinjulu* bird. Dark-red and sinister. Not white and gentle and beckoning, such as Jacinta's were. They instead warned you from a distance: Do not get near me! I can kill! The red eyes partly resulted from the manner in which wizardhood was transferred from one person to another – through the anus. A wizard instructed the prospective initiate to place his naked buttocks on the opening of a burrow in an anthill, to align the anus properly with the opening. Then he went round to the opposite opening of the same burrow and blew the wizardhood, in all its potency, into the burrow. The wizardhood shot through the burrow and rammed into the initiate's anal canal. It was the forceful entry of the malevolent powers of wizardhood that turned the initiate's eyes red. Dark-red. Once this transfer was accomplished, it was next to impossible to reverse it. The recipient of the evil powers was very likely to stay a wizard for life.

'Jacinta,' Olwit said, 'do not take what I am saying lightly. I am already grown up. I want somebody who can keep me company.'

'I know,' Jacinta replied. 'But not everything can happen within one day. No-one can clear a whole garden in only one day, however strong he is.'

'Not when he is using a tractor,' Olwit responded.

Jacinta looked thoughtful for a little while, then spoke. 'All right,' she said. 'But let me tell Albina my friend about what is happening first so that in case anything bad happens to me she knows where to find me.'

And she walked off, pumping and twisting her buttocks as if she had just discovered that she owned a pair of buttocks.

Olwit did not expect Jacinta to return.

Olwit's fear seemed to be justified when he waited for about one hour and she was still nowhere to be seen. He was walking towards the main entrance of the market, intending to go back home, when she showed up. With another girl in tow. She introduced the girl as Albina. Olwit took Albina's appearance in. Short, stout, flat-headed, rough-skinned... And also her gait. Albina lurched from side to side when she walked, like someone who had suffered a heavy jigger infestation as a child.

'I thought you had already given up and left,' Jacinta Apio told Olwit and laughed softly, covering her mouth with both her hands.

'No, I am still around, as you can see,' Olwit answered, not looking too happy. 'Instead I thought that you had left.'

She did not reply. Instead she said, introducing her friend, 'This is Albina.' Then she asked him, 'Are you going home now?'

'No,' Olwit lied.

'Can we come with you?' Jacinta asked.

'Come with me where?' Olwit asked. He was getting quite exasperated with her.

'Wherever you are going,' Albina chipped in.

'All right, come with me,' Olwit said. 'Both of you.'

He took them to Ben Okot's home and bought them two measures of *arege*. He shared the *arege* with them. By the time the girls were through with the liquor, they were giggling like embarrassed nuns.

Both girls accompanied Olwit home that night. Both of them spent the night in Olwit's hut, with Jacinta sharing Olwit's wooden bed and Albina sleeping on a papyrus mat at the foot of the bed.

The following day Albina went back to Aduku, but Jacinta stayed put in Teboke.

Chapter VI

Abudu Olwit had just graduated. He was almost mad with excitement. He had achieved the rare feat of becoming one of only five graduates in Teboke. Abudu Olwit had strutted off into the wider world, his degree in his hand. Four years later, however, he had held three teaching jobs, one in a secondary school and two in commercial colleges, all privately owned. He soon enough discovered that he did not like teaching at all, especially because of the rotten way he was treated by his employers. Now very sober and quite sane, he sought out his parliamentary representative, the Honourable Mike Adoli-Awal.

Like his father before him, Mike Adoli-Awal had been an implacable supporter of the Party of the Palm, TPP. He had been following a very strong family tradition, for whoever had wanted peace in the home of Adoli-Awal's father, Mr Awal the county chief, had to belong to the Party of the Palm. Adoli-Awal's adherence to TPP had been amply rewarded, for during president Bwete's second coming he was appointed Managing Director of the National Manufactory of Shoes and Uniforms, NAMISU. He had also been awarded directorships in various parastatals.

Unlike Mike Adoli-Awal, Abudu Olwit's uncle, Odwong, had belonged to the Party of the Cock, TPC. Right from the time Bwete was president for the first time. And no-one had been able to make him renounce his party. Trying to convert him was as thankless as trying to shave off an ogre's hair – it grew back even as you shaved. Odwong's firm adherence to the Party of the Cock had earned him a number of beatings and lost him a number of friends. But he still stuck with the party. Even during Bwete's second coming when it was anathema in Teboke to belong to a party other than TPP.

Their allegiance to different political parties meant that Mike Adoli-Awal and Odwong detested each other. Adoli-Awal's hatred of Odwong extended to his nephew Abudu Olwit, partly because he felt that Odwong, whom he considered a political renegade, did not deserve a graduate nephew, and partly because he felt that five graduates coming from Teboke meant that university education was getting demystified. It was a typical case of one wanting to be the only cock in the chicken run. And Odwong had only made this hatred more intense by showing Adoli-Awal scant respect. Adoli-Awal had reciprocated by inciting attacks – both physical and verbal – against Odwong. On one occasion two of his grass-thatched huts had been set alight and razed to the ground by Adoli-Awal's political messengers.

When the stool of power was snatched from Bwete for the second time, the enmity between the two men had further deepened. Believing that Odwong would take advantage of Bwete's fall and attempt to hurt him, Adoli-Awal had gone into hiding in Alee village. Odwong had pointed the military agents of General Ragamoi, the new owner of national power, to where Adoli-Awal was hiding. Adoli-Awal had fled like a partridge to Cegere. Odwong had informed General Ragamoi's agents about Adoli-Awal's new hiding-place and they had gone there to look for him, setting him to flight again. This time he had scurried back across Teboke and Alee and on to Aboke, several kilometres away. To Adoli-Awal, Teboke and the neighbouring villages had taken on the very unhelpful dimensions of a hand-woven food-storage bin. You could jump into it, but even when it was empty it would never be able to hide your full height. Your head and shoulders would be hopelessly exposed to full view. In Aboke, Adoli-Awal had decided that it was no longer worthwhile trying to hide on dry land, so he had taken off to Lake Kyoga where he hid on one of the floating islands until the fall of General Ragamoi. Fortunately for Adoli-Awal, General Ragamoi's occupancy of State House was very short-lived, as if the aging general had only made a brief stopover there on his way elsewhere.

Then it was Uchebi's turn to occupy State House. When Adoli-Awal heard that General Ragamoi had lost the stool of power, he stayed put on his floating island, for he was not quite sure which way the wind from Uchebi's new reign would blow. When the insurgency in Apac district flared up, however, Adoli-Awal did not bother to delve into the whys and wherefores of the insurgency. He leapt into it the way a man desperately seeking escape from his pursuers will jump into the first hole he happens upon. The insurgency presented Adoli-Awal with an opportunity to come out of hiding, and it was not an opportunity he was going to miss.

Adoli-Awal survived the insurgency with a minor injury. In an encounter with the new national army, a bullet struck him in the right calf and lodged itself there. He had to wait until the first general amnesty that the new government offered to insurgents before the bullet could be surgically removed. This was two years after the insurgency had started. Soon after he quit the rebellion, Adoli-Awal found himself in the Broadbased National Assembly, the BNA. A year later he was appointed a junior Minister of State.

It was at this point that Abudu Olwit decided to go and see him. Perhaps Adoli-Awal, being a Minister of State, would be able to fix him up with a 'proper' job. Four years out of university and thoroughly fed up with teaching, Olwit very badly wanted a change of job.

Olwit was twenty-eight. Like his mother he was quite short and stocky. Unlike his mother he was not very dark. His mother attributed this to his part-Gisu ancestry, something he hated to hear. Olwit's eyes were wide-set under a broad and high forehead. They were narrow and had little bags under them, and this gave him a squinty look. His nose was short, thin and blunt at the tip. His lips were thick and narrow, with the upper one jutting slightly over the lower, and his chin was narrow and tapered to a sharp point. Because he was thickset and his archless feet pointed inwards, when Olwit walked he waddled like a duck.

Abudu Olwit had arrived in Lira town from Teboke that afternoon. He was tired and very hungry. He did not want the Honourable Adoli-Awal to know that he had walked all the way from Teboke in the sweltering heat, so when Adoli-Awal had asked him by what means he had come to Lira, he had said by bus. Yet his joints ached with tiredness and his stomach growled and rumbled with hunger.

Abudu Olwit had set out for Lira before it was light. He had trudged in his down-at-heel black shoes through the village of Bala, due east from Teboke, then had turned northwards and eastwards again, trekking along narrow paths and broad paths and murram roads, and finally reaching the tarmac road that led into Lira town. Olwit's down-at-heel shoes were only the third pair he had owned since he was born. He had worn the first pair in Senior Three.

63

When he had arrived at the steel gate of Adoli-Awal's home, he had diligently hanky-wiped his dust-coated shoes to a reasonable cleanliness and then pressed the gate bell. A few minutes later, after his identity had been established, he had been allowed into the dignified presence of his parliamentary representative.

'I have looked everywhere for a job, *Adwong*,' was the first thing he had said after greeting the MP, ' but all in vain.' It was one of only a few times since he came down from university that he was addressing someone as *'Adwong'*, a title invested with a great deal of respect and dignity.

His host was seated directly across a lacquered mahogany table from him. He was smoking a Benson and Hedges cigarette. He looked composed and nonchalant. Every now and then he tapped grey ash from the tip of his cigarette into a porcelain ashtray. He seemed to do this unconsciously. As he puffed on his cigarette, Adoli-Awal shot long billows of smoke between pursed lips and through flared nostrils up towards the ceiling of his sitting room. He did not look particularly concerned about what his graduate constituent was telling him. He seemed instead to be interested in the arabesques on the ceiling of his sitting room. His body was slanted across the settee in which he sat, with his left arm flung along its top, like a god in repose.

'I wandered in the streets of Kampala for three years *Adwong*, and nobody even seemed interested enough to ask me my qualifications. I went to Jinja, and things were no better. So I decided to come to you to see if you could help *Adwong,* if you could put in a good word for me here and there...'

Adoli-Awal emitted a long, low sigh that originated from somewhere deep within his guts and travelled up his chest before reaching his nose. Then for the first time he turned and looked at Olwit. He was still seated aslant, and his arm was still draped over the top of the settee back.

'I thought you had a job, Olwit,' he remarked, his eyes squinted, 'a teaching job.'

'You see, *Adwong*,' Olwit explained, 'I have been teaching only in order to wait for a proper job to come up.'

Adoli-Awal sat up, very slowly indeed, and twisted his trunk to the left, then to the right. His back creaked. Then he pinched out his cigarette and gently placed the stub in the ashtray.

'Olwit,' Adoli-Awal said, 'you went to university and read Economics. In Economics you should have studied something to do with starting businesses. Did you not?'

'Yes we did,' Olwit confirmed the obvious.

Later when Olwit thought back to this reply, a reply to something that was obviously meant to be a mockery, coming from someone who had read Economics at university himself, he felt very angry indeed. He wondered what had made him so stupid, what had blocked his sense of smell so effectively that he had not recognised his impending death. For was it not said that what killed a dog first blocked its sense of smell? What had killed his ability to smell death – even his own? Could it have been the ice-cold soda and two sponge cakes the househelp had given him on her master's orders? Why had he not seen his death coming?

'Olwit,' Adoli-Awal said, ' at least you are lucky to have a degree and a job. In fact you should be very thankful for that. As you are still single, you can either save enough money to start a business since you have the training, or you can go back to school and acquire a post-graduate diploma in Education.'

'But *Adwong*,' Olwit protested, 'I never really wanted to be a teacher.'

'Why not?' Adoli-Awal asked.

'Apart from the poor pay, people generally consider teachers to be failures. I do not want to be considered a failure,' Abudu Olwit answered, looking Adoli-Awal straight in the eye.

'So what kind of job do you want to hold? Be a Minister like myself?' As Adoli-Awal asked this question, the left edge of his mouth turned up in scorn.

Olwit ignored the disdain so clearly etched on his parliamentary representative's face. He answered, 'Anything *Adwong*. Any job in government. Any job in a parastatal. Any job so long as it is not cleaning offices or making tea or running errands. Anything, though I would have preferred to work in Revenue Authority, *Adwong*.'

Adoli-Awal responded. 'These are difficult times, my son.' The scorn had not quite left his face yet. 'Jobs are scarce, and good jobs are rare as hen's teeth... Now do me a favour, son.' He was calling him 'son' again. 'If you think you are ashamed of teaching, then I am afraid I cannot help you. Perhaps your uncle Odwong can. Why don't you ask him?'

Adoli-Awal unwound his tall, slender frame from the settee, twisted his trunk to left, then to right. His back creaked. Again. Then he headed for his bedroom. Abudu Olwit did not move. He sat on in the sofa, hoping the kind of hope a dog hopes that has seen the last morsel of meat disappear into its master's mouth. Hoping the kind of hope a dog hopes that has not noticed any bones being placed on the eating table. Hoping the kind of hope a dog hopes that has seen its master punch a hole in the last ball of millet bread, scoop up some soup, eat up the bread and drink up what is still left of the soup. When the househelp showed up several minutes later and gave him three green banknotes and told him: 'This is for your transport back to Teboke,' Olwit was still seated in the bulky sofa hoping the hope of the foolish dog.

Olwit went back to his teaching. A few months later it was announced in the newspapers and on national radio that the government was recruiting university graduates into the Prisons Service at the rank of Assistant Superintendent . The intention of government was to enhance the capacity and performance of the service. Olwit offered himself for recruitment. He was not exactly excited about the possibility of being recruited, but felt that it would at least be a beginning.

Chapter VII

You have probably heard of the Karuma bridge. Or seen it. As you come to the northern end of the bridge, you head towards Corner Kamdini, where the tarmacked road forks into two. The left fork takes you to Gulu town, the most important town in Acholiland, and runs on to Atiak, Adjumani and Sudan. The right-hand branch takes you to Lira, the most important town in Lango, and runs on to Kitgum, and then Sudan.

It is important that you know where Alaro Prison Farm is. So follow the Corner Kamdini-Lira tarmac road. A few kilometres after Corner Kamdini the road bears left and then straightens out after that point. The tarmac road will soon bring you to a cluster of new and old buildings on both of its sides, and a murram road leading off to your right. If you were ill the murram road would take you to St Paul's Hospital, Apicil, one of the oldest, and the best, hospitals in the country. The hospital is owned by the Catholic Church.

Continue along the tarmac until you reach a school on your left that has a chapel in its compound. The chapel is very close to the road and tends to dominate the school. You are now very close to Alaro Prison Farm.

From the point where the school is you will go downhill first, and then uphill, and then downhill again. Just as the road begins to climb again you will see, on your left, beside the road, a metal signpost painted in the colours of the Uganda Prisons Service, that reads:

THE GOVERNMENT OF UGANDA
ALARO PRISON FARM

Just past the signpost is the beginning of a broad murram road that sweeps away towards the jail hemmed in by a chain-link fence.

Around the jail area the prison warders' grass-thatched huts and metal uniports, the prison offices, and the food stores on wooden stilts stand like silent, unmoving sentries. If you stand at the head of this road and face the prison quarters, you will be flanked by a large *owak* tree to your right. The shade of this tree serves as a marketplace where mostly millet beer and foodstuffs are sold. Under this *owak* tree, too, people sometimes get so drunk that it is a miracle they do not get run over by motor vehicles as, numb and stupid with drink, they stagger across the tarmac road. The Alaro Prison Farm staff drink here quite frequently too.

As you look towards the prison buildings, you will see broad sweeps of cotton and maize and soya plants to both your right and left, on both sides of the large murram road leading to the prison. During the busy months of planting, weeding or harvesting of crops you will catch sight of prisoners working between the rows of maize or beans or soya, dipping and rising as they hoe, pick or uproot. The prisoners wear yellow collarless shirts and shorts with drawstring waists without pants. Many of the prisoners look ill-fed and their uniforms are threadbare or tattered. Every now and then you will see one of the prisoners dig one spot repeatedly. He will then proceed to squat down over the hole he has dug and deposit his dung in it. Sometimes with his head in full public view.

Abudu Olwit, Assistant Superintendent of Prisons, Economics graduate of Makerere University, one-time licensed teacher, was the officer-in-charge – or OC – of Alaro Prison Farm. He was thirty-six. He had been posted there five years before.

Abudu Olwit was married to Saida Acola, *Jago* Olima's daughter. Among the locals Olwit was highly respected, and many of them would have offered their daughters to him to become his second, or even third, wife.

***

In primary school, Olwit had had singular difficulties with girls. He had been too diffident and frightened of the girls to have anyone he could call a friend among them. And he had been badly bullied by the boys and older girls. Until one day, pushed beyond endurance, he had stabbed a boy a little older than him with a sharp lead pencil. For this offence he was suspended from school for a term and his mother had to pay two adult goats to the family of the injured boy. Olwit had been in Primary Five then. His shyness and diffidence had, however, not disappeared. And the situation had not improved much when he had entered secondary school.

68

'I do not know when my son will grow into a man,' he one day heard his mother, Alicinora, tell a woman friend of hers. They were seated under a mango tree shelling fresh beans and he was lying in his grass-thatched hut a few metres away. It was May. His mother's voice was raised. Clearly she intended him to hear what she was saying. 'My son just keeps to his hut like a eunuch. He buries his eyes in his books all the time, pretending to be reading. And when he leaves his hut you find him walking alone hither and thither like a wizard. I do not know whether he has friends.

'If he was impotent I would understand. But last year when I abandoned him in anger and went off to my sister Abuli in Agwata he brought a girl here. You might have seen her. Did you?'

'Oh yes,' Alicinora's friend said. 'She was called Akullu. Jacinta Akullu?' Her voice carried a hint of doubt.

'Yes, Jacinta,' Alicinora affirmed. 'But not Akullu. She was called Apio, Jacinta Apio, and she came from Aduku.'

'I remember her quite well,' Alicinora's friend said, 'the slow-walking girl with the soft eyes. She stayed here for some months.'

'Yes, that is the one,' Alicinora confirmed. 'When I returned from Agwata I found the girl here. Olwit had gone back to school and left her here. During the three weeks she had been here alone she had very properly looked after the home. She had very carefully used my beans, peas and simsim. And she had taken very good care of my goats. And not a single one of my chickens had got lost.'

'She was a good girl,' Alicinora's friend remarked. 'She would have made a good wife for him.'

'She was good,' Alicinora confirmed. 'She always listened to me and never raised her voice while speaking to me. And she was very hardworking. And always addressed me as *Ayaa*. I felt very happy being like a mother to her.'

'Mmm,' the friend agreed.

'Then Olwit returns from his Amuka College and asks me what I am still doing with the girl. I ask him in return what he expects me to do after all the trouble he has put me through, being summoned by the sub-county chief and having to pay the elopement fine, which almost swept away all my goats. And the girl not yet even fallen pregnant, though she had told me that my son was all right. So I tell

69

him that if he thinks I will send the girl away, there is something wrong with his head. Do you know what he does?'

'He beats up Jacinta?' the friend enquired.

'No. He tells me that if I have the ability to sleep with Jacinta, I can keep her. As for him, from that day onwards he was not going to enter his hut. Then he transfers to Okaka's home and stays in Okaka's son's hut for the duration of the holidays.'

'Children! When will they ever learn to be grateful to us?' the friend remarked.

'Yet there is no way I could have sent Jacinta away. I did not want to cause trouble for myself with Jacinta's people. Instead I followed Olwit to Okaka's home and quarrelled very hotly with Okaka for taking away my son. I told him that if he did not allow my son to return home I would call lightning down on his home.'

'What did he do?'

'At first he just laughed. Then he told me that if I did not want my son to have an education I could allow him to take him in and keep him in school. I told him that my son could have a wife to help me with work and still have his education. That he could still get even a *digiri*. But the fool would not listen. So I returned home weeping and asked Jacinta to tell her people that my son did not want her any more.

'So she went to Aduku and came back with her father and brothers. They took more of my goats as compensation for the time she had wasted here and went back. Taking her with them.

'And now Olwit spends all his time in that hut of his with his eyes buried in his books like a eunuch. When is he getting me a daughter-in-law?'

Abudu Olwit was in Senior Four then.

***

Later at Makerere University things had been really difficult for Abudu Olwit. The occasional moments of exhilaration could not dispel the general tenor of his feelings: despondency, self-pity, diffidence, inferiority. For one thing, he was broke most of the time. Even with the availability of students' allowances such as 'boom' and book

70

allowance, he could manage only a cheap second-hand Owino Market shirt every now and then. Or Owino Market trousers. Or ties. Or shoes. But coats were out of the question– they were too expensive for him.

One of the most embarrassing moments of his time at Makerere University had been the freshers' ball that the University Guild government had organised to welcome them. He had turned up at the ball in a white poplin shirt, blue gaberdine trousers and black Prefect shoes. Most of the rest of the young men were in designer jeans and T-shirts and running shoes. He had felt very self-conscious. But still he had plucked up the courage to approach two tight-trousered girls chatting with each other and asked one to dance. The girl had not even bothered to look at his face. She had glanced at his cheap Prefect shoes and gaberdine trousers and sniggered, and had continued the conversation with her friend. Olwit had shuffled away from the dance and had comforted himself with two glasses of *kasese* gin. He had never dared attend another Makerere University dance after that.

When Olwit left Makerere University he had not dated any one of the female students, nor did he have a close friend among them. His interactions with them were mostly limited to the lecture room, tutorials, seminars. He did not expect them to be interested in him at all. He felt that there was nothing he could flaunt to try and impress them. He had neither pedigree, nor money, nor nice clothes, nor sporting talent, nor good looks. With money one could take a girl out. With money one could take a girl out and buy her chicken and chips, and a couple of beers. Without money one pretended to have little interest in the girls yet one ogled at the girls' beautiful legs. And if one caught an accidental glimpse of inner university-girl thigh it almost drove one crazy. But one still pretended to be disinterested. And one walked around in one's cheap shoes carrying a stupid aura of indifference around one, thinking anybody cared.

Coming from an obscure village did not help matters either because one did not even have an impressive place to talk about.

- Where do you come from?
- Teboke.

- Teboke? Where's that? In Karamoja?
- No, in Apac.
- What's Apac? A village?
- No, it is a district. And its headquarters is Apac town.
- Oh, I'm so forgetful these days. We learnt about Apac district in primary school. At Kampala Parents'. It is in West Nile, isn't it?
- No, it is not in West Nile. West Nile is very far from Apac district.

And one felt like giving the ignorant little bitch a hard slap on her pouty, lipsticked mouth and dismantling a few of her sparkling pepsodented teeth. But whose fault was it anyway?

Well, Olwit had finished university and received a second-class Economics degree. Without any money to celebrate his achievement. So that he could at least be a star for once in his life.

As Abudu Olwit grappled with university life, Saida Acola was moving up the educational ladder too. A year before Olwit's transfer to Alaro Prison Farm, Saida Acola had finished her course at Uganda College of Commerce, Pakwach, coming down with a Higher Diploma in Marketing.

***

Saida Acola's mother, Bitoroci Alupu, had conditioned her daughter well. Right from the moment she began to understand human speech. And when Saida Acola's womb broke and she started her monthly bleeding, Bitoroci became even more relentless.

'My daughter,' Bitoroci would remind her every now and then, 'you do not marry a man because you love him. You marry a man because he can take care of your needs, because marrying him will make other women envious. It does not matter if he already has a wife. In any case you can be the second or third wife and still dominate your husband.'

All Bitoroci wanted for her daughter was *kuc*. A woman leading a life of *kuc* lived in circumstances of ease, of material abundance. Such a woman experienced peace of mind and physical wellbeing resulting from sufficiency of food, security and her husband's generosity, and from being liked by her husband's people. That was all Bitoroci desired for her daughter. *Kuc!*

In Bitoroci's eyes only rich men counted. The rest might as well have been mere moving shadows. It did not matter that a man was of good family or educated. Whoever ate good family? Whoever ate education? Whoever wore it? Whoever drove around in it? Whoever used it to marry? Her daughter Saida Acola was not going to marry someone who possessed neither car nor cows, someone who could neither build a big *mabati* house nor buy her, Bitoroci, expensive *ikoyi* and *gomici*. If any poor man was intrepid enough to seek her daughter's hand in marriage, she would put him firmly in his place. Poor men were not expected to marry well-raised daughters like her own Saida, but instead to sleep close to their fireplaces to keep their starved and lonely bodies warm.

Bitoroci had put a number of men in their place. And not regretted it, except in one case.

When Saida Acola was in Senior Three in Lira town, Bitoroci had heard that Patrick Amunu of Dr Bwete College and her daughter had started visiting each other frequently, especially on weekends. Soon she began suspecting that they were sleeping with each other.

Now it happened that Patrick Amunu was the son of Okullu Ipapalo. As far back as anyone could remember, Okullu had hawked *ipapalo* – pawpaws – hence his nickname 'Ipapalo'. Even now, in his fifties, he still peddled *ipapalo*. He would ride on his old Gazelle bicycle through Teboke trading centre bellowing *'Ipapalo!... Ipapalo!... Ipapalo!...'* And go on to extol the virtues of his *ipapalo*.

Bitoroci loved Okullu's pawpaws and bought them quite frequently. She despised Okullu and pitied his wife, Katarina. What was wrong with some women, she wondered, hitching yourself to some man who would spend all his life hawking pawpaws and bawling *'Ipapalo!... Ipapalo!...Ipapalo!...'*?

So when Bitoroci learnt that Patrick Amunu had come home for his holidays, she visited him. This was at the end of the term during which she had first heard about their affair. She woke up very early in the morning and rode to Amunu's father's homestead. On the expensive and prestigious Raleigh bicycle that her husband, the sub-county chief, had bought her a few months earlier.

Bitoroci found Amunu still indoors, so she pitched camp in front of Okullu Ipapalo's main house. Okullu Ipapalo had left for the fields a little earlier.

When Katarina, Okullu Ipapalo's wife, came out, she was surprised to find Bitoroci seated on the verandah of her grass-thatched house, next to the entrance door. *Gomici*-ed, her twig-dry legs stretched out in front of her, her chin planted in her right palm. Looking angry and full of spite. Her throat throbbing like a male lizard's.

'*Dyera,* did you sleep well?' Katarina greeted her. Katarina addressed every woman in her age-group as *dyera,* an endearment normally used between women whose children were married to each other.

'Do not deafen my ears with this talk of *dyera*,' Bitoroci spat. 'Since when did you become my *dyera*?'

Katarina reared back with shock at her visitor's rudeness.

'*Imat* Bitoroci,' she responded, 'I have never known you behave this way before. Is there a problem?'

'Yes,' Bitoroci answered, firmly. 'I do have a problem with your son, Amunu. And I want to speak to him now. And if he is still sleeping, the lazybones, you had better rouse him and tell him.'

Bitoroci's throat pulsed.

'*Imat* Bitoroci,' Katarina said, 'what has my son done that you should want to talk to him so early in the morning?'

'You should know,' Bitoroci retorted. 'You cannot pretend not to know what has been going on between your son and my daughter all this time. In any case, I came to talk to him, not to you!'

Katarina stood around for some time, glaring at Bitoroci. Bitoroci glared right back. Then Katarina spoke. 'All right,' she said, 'I will call him for you.' And she stalked away towards Amunu's grass-thatched hut tucked a few metres away behind the main house. A few minutes later she re-appeared, with a sleepy-eyed Amunu in tow. The moment Bitoroci saw Amunu, she reared up from her perch on the verandah, her eyes narrowed and dark with venom.

Amunu arrived where Bitoroci was and positioned himself in front

74

of her.

'Look at him,' she spat, 'so lazy he has to be woken by his mother when the sun is already up. And he thinks I can allow him to marry my daughter! *Cede!*' And she spat a spray of saliva on the ground to her left. Amunu glanced at his mother, and then back at Bitoroci. Amunu was in Senoir Five, tall, dark, athletic. He was eighteen.

Bitoroci glared at him, her eyes dark with derision. 'Look how he looks at his mother,' she said. 'At your age you still think your mother should always be around to give you support, eh? And you think you are a man!' Then she barked out a laugh. Just once. Eh-hey!

Amunu glanced at his mother again. Then he looked back at Bitoroci. His tongue was as heavy as a grinding stone. His face began to convulse.

'And now his face twitches like that of a hen thief!' Bitoroci chided. 'Tell me, young man. Tell me what you have been doing with my daughter! Tell me now! Tell me!' And her hands clenched hard.

'*Imat* B-B-Bitoroci,' Amunu stuttered, rubbing his palms together, '*Imat* Bito –'

'He does not even know how to be polite to his mother's agemates,' Bitoroci cut in, 'rubbing his palms together like a praying mantis. When we were still young, we were expected to keep our hands behind our backs while talking to an elder. Not rub them together in front of us as if we were begging for money!'

Amunu transferred his hands behind his back and looked down. His face twitched even worse.

Amunu had always been frightened of Bitoroci. Of her hacksaw voice, her acid eyes, her scorpion tongue. He had never thought he would ever be the target of her rage until her daughter had taken an interest in him. She was the one who had started it all by sending him a hand-embroidered handkerchief scented with talcum powder. And now he was being insulted like a common thief!

Bitoroci picked up where she had left off. 'Now, young man, let me tell you one thing,' she announced. 'No daughter of mine is going to marry the son of a man who is good only at hawking pawpaws and who does not possess even a single cow. And who lives in a smelly, run-down, grass-thatched house!'

And Bitoroci started moving towards her gleaming black-and-silver Raleigh bicycle parked right in the middle of Okullu Ipapalo's compound. Katarina's voice, however, cut her progress short. Bitoroci spun around to face Katarina.

'Bitoroci,' Katarina said, 'I thought you had a quarrel with my son alone. Do not include us his parents in your quarrel, let me tell you. My husband may be an unimportant man who only sells pawpaws, but it is because of those pawpaws that our son is in secondary school. It is also because of those pawpaws that he has been sleeping with your daughter.'

Bitoroci's eyes widened, then narrowed. Her chest heaved. Her male-lizard neck throbbed even harder.

'Katarina,' she said, 'your son may sleep with my daughter now but he will not marry her. After all, of all the people you slept with only one married you. And you chose the worst of the lot. Perhaps because you are so ugly.'

Katarina laughed. Eh-hey! 'Look who is talking about ugliness,' she countered. 'I wonder whether *Jago* Olima married you with his eyes closed, what with your stiff and skinny neck and dry twiggy legs. No wonder no single man would take you, so you had to settle for an old married man.'

Bitoroci swallowed a ball of saliva. Then she spoke. 'Old he may be,' she said, ' but I was not going to marry a worthless pawpaw seller who lives in a grass-thatched hut crawling with mice.'

Katarina's face had grown stormy. 'Get out of my compound,' she screamed, 'before I break your thin neck!' Then she dashed into the kitchen.

Bitoroci scrambled for her bike, mounted it. She had just started peddling away when Katarina emerged from the kitchen wielding a thick wooden pestle above her head with both hands. She chased after Bitoroci's bike for a few metres and then hurled the pestle. It landed a few feet short of the rear wheel of the bike. Katarina cursed in disappointment. Then she broke down and wept.

Amunu sighed, then went behind a bushy shrub to urinate.

When Okullu Ipapalo learnt about what Bitoroci thought about him from his wife, he did not sell pawpaws that day. Instead, the moment he had washed himself after work, he went off to drink at Teboke trading centre, where Bitoroci lived. And drank until dark. And got drunk. But just drunk enough to be bitingly articulate. Then he strolled up the main street of Teboke trading centre once. And down it once too. While shouting at the top of his lungs:

Jo okene kobo ni	Some people say that
An konya pe	I am worthless
Pien ni an acato	Because I sell
Ipapalo!	Pawpaws!
Aco wan dang orom!	Yet we are all equal!
Aco jono ngut-gi	Those people have
Dang orwaye	Thin, long necks
Tyen-gi dang	And their legs are
Tino, otwoo	Tiny, dry
Neno gi dang rac!	They are ugly
	To look at!

After launching his insults into the night, Okullu Ipapalo went back to his home. And never sold pawpaws to Bitoroci again. Nor to any member of her household.

Patrick Amunu went on to train as a doctor in Israel. By the time Saida Acola got married to Abudu Olwit, Amunu had become a respected paediatrician. Saida Acola still had a soft spot for him, and considered her marriage to Abudu Olwit as something of a social climb-down. Her own mother Bitoroci never quite forgave herself for treating the young man the way she did.

Chapter VIII

Silence. It was a deep and disturbing silence in the ginnery. A silence broken only occasionally by the chattering of bats and the shrieks of little children playing among the dismantled and scattered machinery, or on the rusting, flat-tyred, old-fashioned trucks.

Most of the ginnery buildings still stood. The concrete and *mabati* walls were still strong. But most of the machinery had either been carted away or put out to be attacked by sun and rain.

Inside the ginnery buildings the smell of rotting cotton was strong. It choked you with its mustiness, tickled your nose and made you sneeze. Achyaa!! But if you sniffed around more carefully you would notice two other smells. One the smell of bat waste, and the other that of children's dung. The latter warm and sour-sweet, rising up from the floor of the dead ginnery in steamy waves. The children preferred to deposit their dung in the dark inner corners of the buildings, sneaking in and laying the dung carefully down in little steamy mounds. The children rarely played inside the buildings.

Some of the buildings had been pulled down by the ginnery owners before their departure for other lands. It was on the floors of these buildings that the children played. They built little flat cars out of salvaged bits of timber and ball-bearing casings. The ball-bearing casings served as wheels. The front wheels were mounted on the ends of a stout piece of wood and fixed to the bottom of the car with only one long nail so that the car could turn corners. And the children sat on the cars and were pushed around by other children. With a long, forked stick and at top speed. And the feet of the 'driver' would be planted firmly on the front 'axle' close to the two wheels, to steer the car. The children shrieked with delight as they 'drove' the cars.

The broken-down lorries, almost all of them without engines, were parked side-by-side just inside what used to be the main gate. Big, ugly, timber-backed lorries with tapering snouts and large, bulging mudguards and bench seats. The children played on the lorries too. They got behind their steering wheels and 'drove' them, twisting the large steering wheels right and left, making loud, shrill lorry noises with their mouths.

78

When the ginnery was closed and dismantled, its Indian owners, Hippen and Ramchand, had become very rich indeed. Ikangi, whom the locals had by now established was the cashier, but whose origins were still being hotly debated, had become quite prosperous too. And very fat, like a traditional Lango chief. He looked as if he had swallowed a soft, shifting waterpot, and was hiding an earthenware bowl somewhere beneath his tongue. His sleek, drooping stomach had drunk away his buttocks, so that they had become as flat as those of Ramchand's wife, Arundhati.

Immediately after the closure of the ginnery, Ikangi had departed from Teboke with his wife, his two daughters and three sons. It was said that he had gone to Buganda to take up a bigger job in a bigger cotton ginnery there. Some people however refuted this, insisting that he had set up a very big shop in Masindi town and now drove an expensive Zephyr instead of the cheap little Volkswagen Beetle, or 'Tortoise', that he used to own. Nobody was, however, sure.

Those who had worked on the ginnery floor were at a loss where to go. They slouched around Teboke looking for odd jobs, sometimes getting them from the Arab shopkeepers and restaurant owners, sometimes from the richer locals, but most times getting nothing. They were a lost lot, looking subdued and muddled-up like a kitten that lost its mother at birth. There was Gaiteng, for example, who had come from Koboko in the north-west of Uganda and who was killed by jiggers that burrowed into his toes and fingers and heels and soles and buttocks and manhood, so that his body was a mass of throbbing pain. He died lying on his belly, his body raw and bleeding from soiled, broken-nailed scratching. And there was Cheptot from Sebei, who had taken to digging pit latrines when he lost his ginning job. One latrine pit almost buried him alive when one of its walls collapsed on him, breaking his right arm and three of his right ribs. After the fractures had healed, Cheptot left Teboke for his home district, Sebei, and was never heard of again.

The ginnery had died but its spirit still lived among Teboke folk. People still heard its sounds in their heads. They still remembered, and often missed, those who had worked in the ginnery but who, since its closure, had gone back where they had come from or proceeded to other districts. With their departure Teboke had become

79

·a little sadder, a lot duller, for few of the locals could match the riotous, boisterous ways of the ginnery workers. People still talked about Ikangi and his mysterious ways and origins, and about how the ginnery used to sing about him. And the many young women who had had boyfriends among the ginnery workers missed them badly, for men were in very short supply now.

Five years after Ikangi's departure Teboke folk were surprised to see one of Ikangi's daughters, Irene Namu, walking down the main street of Teboke trading centre. It was early afternoon. Irene, the younger of the two daughters that Ikangi had, had matured into a quiet-spoken, amiable, bright-eyed young woman with dimples in her cheeks. She had become plump and her light skin glowed with good eating. The arrogance of her adolescent years had vanished. She laughed easily, throwing her head back and freely giving vocal expression to her mirth. And she laughed like a typical Lango woman. Eh-hey! Eh-eh-eh-hey! And she seemed to take great delight in simply being alive and in meeting people.

The afternoon Irene Namu turned up after her absence of five years, she met a lot of people.

'Kelementi, how have you been doing?'

'Really well. You can see I have not aged a bit. How is my friend Ikangi?'

'He is getting on quite well. Only he has chased away my mother and married a younger woman.'

***

'Namu, you have grown up into a very beautiful woman. Will you marry my son?'

Namu's eyes get even brighter with mirth before she speaks. 'Jucumeri, why do you ask me on his behalf? Why don't you take me to see him first? Perhaps he has lost all his teeth during the time I have been away.'

And the two women laugh together. Eh-hey!

***

80

'Irene, I almost failed to recognise you. Do you still speak Lango?'
'Oh yes! My Lango is actually better than yours. Eh-hey!'
'And I hope you still drink *acoi* beer. Will you join us?'
'Certainly. But I will not stay long. I am looking for Obong.
Once I find him, I shall be on my way to Lira.'
'Will you come back?'
'Yes. Next week. I intend to settle here.'
'That will be good.'

***

After meeting Michael Obong, Irene Namu proceeded to Lira town that same day. A week later she returned to Teboke and set up a bar-restaurant at Teboke trading centre, opposite Opio-Tali's shop.

Chapter IX

At first everybody wondered. Suddenly Bitoroci, Saida Acola's mother, began to visit Alicinora, Abudu Olwit's mother, in her home. Frequently. Yet for years she had not had a single nice thing to say about Alicinora. They also began drinking *kwete* and *arege* together, and were to be seen moving around the nearby Loro market together quite frequently on Fridays. And they had started addressing each other as *dyera*. *Dyere* was a friendship, a close relationship, resulting from marriage between the children of two people, or two homes. At times a marriage brought together two clans that had walked parallel paths, and thus established *dyere* between them. The parties to this sort of relationship addressed one another as *dyera*, 'my-very-close-friend-by-marriage'.

It did not take long for Teboke folk to know about the origins of the close friendship between Bitoroci and Alicinora. They soon learnt that Bitoroci's daughter, Saida Acola, spent most of her vacations from the Uganda College of Commerce, Pakwach, with Abudu Olwịt. Furthermore, Bitoroci presently started bragging that her daughter had caught herself an *opica*. Such was how anyone in an important government job was called, *opica* – 'officer.' Bitoroci bragged that the *opica* would soon marry her daughter. Alicinora, on her part, was delighted at the prospect of having the daughter of a *gombolola* chief become her daughter-in-law, she who had been treated worse than a dog for so many years.

'People used to think that I would die like a dog,' she would tell whoever cared to listen, 'without anyone to take care of me in my old age. Now my son is an *opica*, and is marrying *Jago* Olima's daughter.'

Alicinora was proud too that her son had acquired a *digiri*. As far as she was concerned, that meant that he was more knowledgeable than everyone else in Teboke and all the neighbouring villages, except those who had been to Makerere University like Abudu Olwit himself. Of course there were only three university graduates besides Olwit and Mike Adoli-Awal. She, like many Teboke folk, did not believe that Fr Guglielmo Varasco had been to university, for it

82

was said that the priest's English, both spoken and written, was very simple and quite often ungrammatical. Anyone who had been to university was expected to construct long, complex sentences and intersperse their speech with heavy, baffling words. If they did not do that they were suspected not to have gone to their respective 'Makereres', whether the Ugandan one or the ones found in other countries.

Abudu Olwit's marriage to Saida Acola had not been a simple thing. Apart from the *aranga* money, which is the first instalment of the cash component of the bridewealth, and which the prospective bride is supposed to keep, Olwit had to raise a number of other items. Consequently he had married quite expensively.

Saida Acola's father, *Jago* Olima, had not minced words about the material value of his daughter. 'My son,' he had addressed Olwit, leaning back into his comfortable deck chair, 'you have come hunting in my home and have speared your quarry. That is fine. But I would like to remind you that my daughter is neither uneducated nor an *akopi*. So before you can take her away we shall expect you to show real appreciation for the way we raised her.'

After he had paid the second cash instalment of the bridewealth, Abudu Olwit and his folks and friends were invited to *Jago* Olima's home and presented with a list of what he was expected to hand over to his in-laws before his marriage could be considered complete:

Six new Lango hoe-blades.
Two chickens.
One twenty-pack carton of Sportsman cigarettes.
One twenty-pack carton of Supermatch cigarettes.
Two spear-blades.
Fifteen cows.
Twelve goats.

Olwit's intermediary looked through the list and passed it on to Olwit. In silence. Olwit's eyes moved down the list, and when he reached the cows and goats he gasped. He was being asked for fifteen cows and twelve goats at a time when, following the waves of rustling and destruction by Karimojong and other cattle thieves, the most a man could reasonably be expected to pay was three cows and six goats, the latter having been the standard for the last several

83

years. He knew that the number of animals demanded was meant to form the basis of negotiation, but it was also a rough indicator of how many the bride's people were willing to accept. Nobody who asked for fifteen cows and twelve goats would settle for anything less than eight cows and ten goats. Olwit and his delegation negotiated hard and managed to beat his father-in-law's delegation down to seven cows and eight goats. He had the goats – in fact he possessed a few more goats than the eight. As for the cows, however, he would have to look for the money to buy more of them since he owned only three.

When Abudu Olwit completed his marriage to Saida Acola, she was already pregnant with their first child.

***

Alaro Prison Farm was a large and busy place and Saida's mother, Bitoroci, was a frequent visitor to Abudu Olwit's home at the farm. One would expect to see her there every other Friday. She would ride the eight kilometres from Teboke to Loro market, on her Raleigh bicycle. At the market she would buy a few things, drink a little and then proceed to Alaro Prison Farm. Often in the late afternoon. She would stay at the farm until Sunday and then return home. Often with a small present given her by her daughter, or her son-in-law, strapped with a rubber band to the carrier of her bike.

On returning to Teboke, Bitoroci would boast a lot. She would tell whoever asked her where she had been 'lost' to: 'I went to see Saida on Friday. Both she and her husband did not want me to leave. "*Imat*, stay another day," they insisted. But I said, "Aah, my children, let me go. I have left plenty of work at home." And they gave me this little bundle to bring home.'

Most of the prisoners at Alaro Prison Farm knew Saida Acola. They called her 'Mama OC' in deference to her husband's position as the officer-in-charge of Alaro Prison Farm. In their malnourished, sex-starved misery and endless boredom, some of them ardently desired her tall, lithe body. Of course there were other women on the prison farm too: the wives of the prison officers, their daughters, women living with the prison officers' families. But there was something so haughty about Mama OC's small-stepped gait and

84

large-eyed, thin-nosed, distant countenance that some of the prisoners thought it would be interesting to find out whether she was really haughty all the time, even inside the darkness of a sleeping hut. Many of the prisoners fantasised about her as they sought relief through the agency of their hands, or when another man accepted, or was forced, to play the role of a woman in the darkness of a jail uniport.

Dark, tall, slender and long-necked, Saida Acola nibbled the ground with her feet when she walked. Like a rabbit eating a piece of potato vine. She had copied this gait from the pictures of white women she had seen on TV, tall, thin women with seductive eyes who took rapid, infinitesimal steps as they wafted by in their trench coats, high-slit ankle-length skirts or micro-minis.

Abudu Olwit had set aside one red Massey Ferguson tractor for his personal use. The tractor worked on the portion of the prison farmland that he had allotted to himself. It also fetched water and firewood for him, and sometimes ferried Alaro folks to markets, burials, funerals, marriage feasts and other important occasions. The other two tractors, another red Massey Ferguson and a green four-wheel-drive Deutz, did the prison work proper. Though a large part of the farmland had been allotted to the warders and officers, including the Farm Manager, still a lot of it was left over. The two tractors roared and jerked over the strips of land allocated for prison use, turning the rich dark soil over, digging up roots and often snakes, giant rats and mole rats, sometimes slicing them into little bits of quivering flesh.

The prisoners were always woken up by 5 a.m. One of the warders on duty would strike the lorry-rim bell hung from a tree branch with a long steel bar. The warders seemed to have been trained to strike the bell the same way, for the way they struck it always followed the same pattern. Tang---Tang-tang---Tang-tang-taang---Tang--- On hearing the bell, the prisoners would scramble up from their sleeping mats. Then they would dash water onto their faces and proceed to squat down in rows so they could be counted before being given farm implements and herded away to the fields. Those among them who valued their teeth would break off twigs from the bushes and saplings they came upon, chewing their tips into soft bristles and using them to clean their teeth.

If they were lucky, before they trudged off to the fields they would each receive a cup of a thin, sugarless maize gruel. Their work started at the break of dawn and went on until 1.00 p.m., when a halt would be called and they would eat lunch. Lunch consisted almost invariably of bean sauce and maize *ugali*. The prisoners would resume work an hour later and go on up to 5.00 p.m. They would then be ordered to line up, be counted again and marched back to the jail. At the jail they would wash up, eat their supper, be ordered to fall into line. Then they would be counted yet again and commanded to get into their uniports, where they would be locked up for the night.

The senior prison officers allotted themselves prisoners to work in their homes and gardens. Such prisoners did the dishes and the laundry, ironed the clothes, split firewood, cooked, and sometimes bathed the officers' children. Those who worked in the officers' gardens planted the crops, weeded them, stooked them, and frequently carried the harvest to the homes of the officers. This category of prisoners were usually rewarded for their services. They were frequently given food, drinks and tobacco, and the freedom to roam around the prison officers' living quarters. The other prisoners envied and resented them, for they considered them a privileged lot. But none of them would dare attack them, for attacking them would lead to dire consequences since they enjoyed the special protection of the officers for whom they worked. From what had happened before, the less privileged prisoners knew what kinds of punishment that kind of behaviour could draw.

Not so long ago, a soldier, Corporal Lolo, who was on remand for rape, had started a quarrel with one of the 'privileged' prisoners and broken his head with a piece of split firewood. It was 2.00 p.m. on a Sunday, a day of rest even for the prisoners. Corporal Lolo had been put in solitary confinement right away. The following morning he had been ordered by a gun-wielding warder to dig a big hole in an anthill full of termites. Then the warder had tied his hands behind his back and ordered him to crawl into the hole he had dug – and stay in the hole until 5.00 p.m. Corporal Lolo had got in feet first. It was

86

12.30 p.m. The termites had started attacking him even before his feet touched the back of the hole. His howls of pain and desperate pleas for pardon had fallen on deaf ears. Instead the warder had cocked his AK 47 and kept him under armed guard, with the nozzle of the rifle trained on his shaven head. When Corporal Lolo was ordered out of the hole about five hours later, his body was covered with red soil and blood from termite bites.

But Corporal Lolo was particularly unfortunate that day. He had been put in the hands of a warder who was widely known for his heartlessness. As the warder was escorting the army corporal back to the jail, they happened on a long line of vicious, stinking *kalalang* ants. The warder ordered the soldier, whose hands were still bound behind his back, to fall down and roll over them. The soldier refused. The warder tripped him up and kicked him repeatedly as he tried to get away from the nasty insects that were now stinging him on all the exposed parts of his body. Some had even worked their way inside his old yellow prison uniform. When Corporal Lolo finally managed to get up despite the kicks, he ran stumbling back to the jail, his entire body throbbing with pain.

Corporal Lolo was ill for a week but was not allowed to receive medical treatment. Fortunately, he did not die.

The prisoners at Alaro Prison Farm were a varied lot. There was Odida-Jai, for example, who had been convicted of manslaughter after he had chased and speared to death a man whom he caught dragging away one of his goats on a Christmas night. There was also Wala, a boy of seventeen, who had beaten up his businessman father for refusing to pay his school fees. He was convicted for assault and causing grievous bodily harm, and had been in jail for one year now. He mostly supplied drinking water to his fellow prisoners in the fields. Then there was Opio-Tuma who was on remand for arson. When the *askaris* from the local sub-county headquarters had combed the villages under their jurisdiction for graduated tax defaulters, they had found Opio-Tuma hiding among groundnuts and millet in one of the mud-and-wattle granaries in his compound. He was not a tax defaulter, and they had not been looking for him but instead his younger brother, whom they suspected he had given sanctuary to. Opio-Tuma had neither been seen nor heard of for a month so the *askaris* thought he had run away. When they happened on him, the *askaris* promptly arrested him and later turned him over to the police at Atura Police Station.

Opio-Tuma had burnt down Apollo Uma's main house on the grounds that Uma had killed two of his children using witchcraft. The children, one five and the other three years old, and both boys, had died within a week of each other after eating ripe *amemmo* bananas that they had stolen from Uma's garden.

Opio-Tuma and Apollo Uma had not been on good terms from the time, two years earlier, when they had gone to court over land. Apollo Uma felt, and made it widely known, that the court's decision had not been fair since part of the land court had awarded to his neighbour, Opio-Tuma, actually belonged to him. When his children ate the *amemmo* bananas and died, therefore, Opio-Tuma concluded that Apollo Uma had killed them in revenge for what he considered the court's unfairness.

Each year Abudu Olwit remitted only about half of the proceeds from the sale of Alaro Prison Farm crops to Prisons Headquarters. The rest of the money he split with his Farm Manager and his superiors. He also regularly put in requisitions for uniforms and other items for his prisoners but the bulk of the money ended up in his pocket. Within two years of his posting to Alaro Prison Farm, Abudu Olwit had bought a pick-up and two mini-buses that served as taxis on the Corner Kamdini-Kigumba route. The people of Alaro considered Olwit a very wealthy man. Saida Acola openly bragged about her husband's achievements and treated the prisoners who worked in her home with shrill-voiced and open contempt.

Chapter X

That year was bad. It was a very bad year for Teboke and the surrounding villages. It was a year of hunger, of tying a cloth around your stomach so that you did not feel the hunger too much. It was a year of putting off of marriages because you did not wish to feed your new bride on mangoes and wild greens. It was also a year of death.

That year the rains had taken people by surprise. Suddenly the sky had become dark and heavy with clouds. Then the clouds had burst and soaked the fields with their life-giving waters. Rain. It fell day after day, for hours each day. Sometimes it fell during the day, sometimes at night. Thunder crashed and lightning flashed, sending children screaming with fright. Sometimes the rain would stop suddenly and the rainbow would appear in a giant arc of mesmerizing colours. The children would talk about its beauty and about how your skin would peel off if you passed through it. Had it not happened to Jovino Odongo who went to the woods on the fringes of Okole swamp to cut trees to build himself a new house? Had he not walked through the rainbow without knowing and a few days later patches of pink had begun to appear on his skin, starting with his face? Now look how his lips had become pink. And his arms and his legs. And the eyelids too. And how his eyelashes now looked like those of the pink type of large pig that Acanga Guy had brought from Bala village. Grey like an old man's.

That year rain had swooped down from the skies and made the ground wet and good for planting. The farmers had made the soil ready to receive the seeds and had planted beans and millet and groundnuts and maize and potatoes. Digging little holes in the ground and depositing seeds in them. Or casting the seeds on the ground and turning the soil over with Lango hoes. Or building large mounds of soil and sticking pieces of potato vine in their tops and sides.

And the people were happy.

And they drank and sang.

And they talked about the big harvests they would gather in... and about the bicycles they would buy...and the big radio cassettes... and the foam mattresses.

89

The groundnuts, beans, millet and maize came up, tender and swollen and dark-green with health. The leaves on the potato vines withered, then new ones sprouted to take their place. All green or purple or mottled green-and-yellow. And they too healthy, and nestling against the mounds of earth like a baby against the curve of its mother's breast. Every day the groundnuts, beans, millet and maize grew a little taller, a little thicker, and they got a little closer to the farmers' mouths. The potato leaves left the comfort and protection of the mother-mounds and stood erect and confident and strong.

Then the sun struck. Day after day, it stung the ground with its relentless heat. It sucked up the water in the ground and the lazy wind carried it away on its gentle back. It baked the ground hard, shrinking it, cracking it in parts like the back of a barbecued *obago* rat. The thirsty soil wrapped itself hard around the roots of the millet, and the groundnuts, and the beans and the potato vines, and stifled them. Half-dead, with nothing to eat and nothing to drink, they first hung their heads towards the ground, limp and weak with thirst and hunger, the strong green colour seeping slowly out of them, leaving a sickly yellow in its place. Then the plants lay down on their sides and backs and bellies and they died a slow, thirsty, pale-yellow death.

Still sometimes the sky turned dark with the massing of large clouds and the people began to hope. But the clouds took a long, leisurely walk across the sky and let off the rain they contained elsewhere. Most of the time, however, the sky was smooth, hard and grey as flint. And it sent down a sharp, harsh heat that broiled people's brains and made their hunger worse.

During this period those who had mature cassava in their gardens became 'chiefs'. They exchanged the cassava for the few chickens and ducks and goats and sheep that the people still possessed and sometimes bartered it for sex with women who had nothing else to offer. Those who bought the cassava ate it with greens gathered from the bush, or with partridge, guinea fowl, dove or even crested crane killed with poison . The more enterprising people rode their bicycles to Atura village, where there was no drought and famine, to fetch cassava from there. And *arege*.

90

Not everyone, however, bought the cassava, even those who could. Some instead raided the cassava gardens, especially at night, and stole what amount they could. Sometimes they carried pangas or spears against the possibility of being caught stealing the cassava by the owners of the gardens.

Still, bought or stolen, the cassava was not nearly enough to fill one's stomach. Nor was the sauce. For people used to eating large quantities of *kwon kal* – millet bread – and bean or pigeon-pea sauce, it was very painful to make do with measly amounts of food that merely squatted on the bottoms of plates and bowls.

And the people got hungrier and hungrier. And the hunger and the heat made them listless and mad.

Then the disease that killed people within a few days of catching it came down from Abyssinia. A week after the government had warned people about its rapid spread, five people were dead. Three men and two women. They had all been to the popular Friday Loro market and had died within a few days of each other. They all died the same way. They suffered from headache and fever, and they vomited a lot. They were said to have died of stiff-neck disease, named thus because the skull-splitting headache and the fever made it difficult for one who had caught it to turn one's head. And they were said to have caught the disease at Loro market. Loro market at once became very unpopular indeed.

About a month after the death of the five, another seven people died. They had attended the burial of an old man, and when they returned home they too complained of headaches and felt feverish. They died vomiting.

The government warned people against gathering in large groups so as to limit the spread of the disease.

'How can the government expect us not to gather together in these hard times and yet that is the only way we can comfort one another?' the people complained.

'God is angry with us!' the more Christian ones among them remarked. 'Look what he is doing to us. First he sent us the *thin* disease, and now this stiff-neck disease!'

The *thin* disease had already killed a number of Teboke folk. If you were slender people only noticed that your health was bad when

91

the veins in your arms and legs began to stand out like beer-drinking tubes. And when the hollows behind your collar bones deepened, sometimes becoming deep enough to hold water. Then they knew that you were about to die. But your worsening health would not have been as easy to notice as that of someone who was fat. The speed at which the disease wasted away a fat person was terrifying. It first made him trim, then thin, and then it ate him up. Well, there was nothing one could do about the *thin* disease anyway.

But this new disease, stiff-neck disease, could be treated, they had been told. In hospital. But who had enough money to take a patient to the Catholic hospital, St Paul's Hospital Apicil? When they barely had money to buy food? And government hospitals were bad, for you went there only to lie around on their beds, or even on a mat laid on the floor of a ward, as if you did not have a place to lie down in your own home!

Then somebody brought them great news. In Aduku, a few miles away, stiff-neck disease was being treated with liniment. You made small cuts on your neck with a razor blade and rubbed the liniment into the cuts. Or you drank the liniment. Suddenly all the shops in Teboke were stocked with liniment. And almost everybody was making cuts on their necks, and even foreheads, and rubbing liniment into them. And some were drinking it. Even if the little pain you felt in your neck came from sleeping too long on only one side of your body, you went for the liniment treatment. If your throbbing headache came from an *arege* hangover, you knew how to deal with it. You used liniment. Suddenly everyone discovered that they were ill and liniment became a family lotion, an everyday beverage. People smeared themselves with liniment, rubbed liniment into their sores, sipped liniment, talked liniment, dreamt liniment.

It became routine for Fr Guglielmo Varasco to appeal to God to relieve his flock of distress. Every Sunday he pleaded with his Lord, sometimes sounding quite desperate. Lord, he would frequently pray, if you cannot send down the rain, at the very least stop the stiff-neck disease from killing my people. Even when you punished your own chosen people, the Israelites, you knew when to stop. Whatever the transgressions of my flock, oh Lord, forgive them too.

But still more people died of stiff-neck disease.

The elders of Teboke, Alee, Abolo, Agong, Olo-lango and all the other nearby villages called a meeting. In the meeting they decided to send a delegation to a diviner to find out why their villages were suffering one misfortune after another. Had somebody perhaps committed the abomination of burying a dead dog instead of leaving it to rot out in the open? If not, why had the rains departed so suddenly and refused to return? Why had the *thin* disease been sent among them? Was it not meant to be a disease only of big towns such as Kampala, Jinja and Entebbe? Look how many young people were dying of the disease! And now the stiff-neck disease that some people claimed had come down from Abyssinia – why had it passed the lands of the Karimojong and Iteso and Kumam and Acholi and settled in Lango if it had not been sent?

So the elders elected a delegation from among themselves to visit *Ojee* Penakaci Opige. A delegation of six elderly men.

Penakaci Opige was one of the most famous, and most highly respected, diviners and medicine men in Lango. It was said that most of his divinations were accurate.

When the delegation of elders arrived, they found Penakaci Opige in his divination hut. The moment they greeted him, he told them that he had been expecting them and bade them sit down. Then he belched richly – like a well-fed polygamist – before draping a leopard skin across his right shoulder and picking up his gourd rattle. He raised the rattle above his head and shook it. Three times. Kwara-kwara-kwara-kwara--- Kwara-kwara-kwara-kwara--- Kwara-kwara-kwara-kwara. He was summoning his chief spirit, Acuman.

Even in the harsh light of mid-afternoon, it was very dark inside Opige's divination hut.

Opige spoke, addressing himself to the chief spirit: 'Acuman!'

'Eeh,' a voice came down from the top of the fork-tipped central support of the hut. The six elders glanced up but could not see anyone.

'Acuman, I have some visitors here,' Penakaci Opige announced.

'I have seen them,' Acuman responded from his perch. 'They are six, and their eyes are filled with worry. I greet you all, my fellow elders.'

'We greet you too,' the elders replied, in unison.

'I am happy you have come to see me,' Acuman said.

'We thank you for saying that.'

Acuman's voice was deep and vibrant. A man's voice.

'What gifts have you brought for me?' Acuman enquired.

'We have only brought two white hens and a black ram.'

The spirit laughed from his perch above the elders. A deep, long, sonorous laugh. Then it spoke. 'If you have brought me only those, then you are not true elders. I am an old man with few good teeth. I can only eat so much meat. But I love a good drink, especially *arege*. Have you brought me some *arege*?'

The elders glanced at one another before one of them responded. 'We forgot,' he said, 'but we can send for it. If there is anyone to send.'

The elders took up a collection and placed the banknotes on an old enamel saucer placed at the foot of the central roof support.

The diviner called out across the compound to his wife: 'Olyeekooo!' She was in their small grass-thatched kitchen.

'Eeee!' she responded, and shortly afterwards stood in the door of the kitchen.

'Come!' Penakaci Opige commanded.

When Olyeko came into the divination hut, Opige passed the saucer to her.

'Go buy a bottle of *arege* for Acuman,' he ordered.

She emptied the money into her palm, placed the saucer back at the foot of the roof support and walked back into her kitchen. A few moments later she came out holding a Martini bottle and turned into a path that ran past the side of the main house.

When Olyeko returned with the *arege*, Penakaci Opige poured out a glass of it and placed it next to the saucer at the foot of the roof support.

'Acuman!' he called out.

'I have heard,' Acuman replied.

'Here is your drink.'

'I have seen it.'

94

Then, as everybody watched, the level of the *arege* in the glass began to go down. Then it did not go down any further. Soon after, a sigh of satisfaction was heard at the top of the roof support: 'Aah! That *arege* was good. I thank you for buying it for me, my fellow elders.'

'We accept your thanks,' the elders replied.

The problems of life had become too heavy for the elders to carry alone, Acuman said, so they wanted someone who could make the problems seem lighter. Look, there was the drought. The sun had become very fierce and vengeful. As if someone had insulted its mother. Now people were hungry. In his frequent travels he had seen very many folk whose clothes had become too large for them. Some of the men had to tie strings around their waists so as to keep their shorts and trousers in place. He had also seen many women with bands of cloth around their waists, tied very tightly to make them feel the hunger a little less sharply. People could not make children anymore, for where would one get the strength to do that from? Most of the men who had intended to marry wives that year had put off their marriages, for what would you feed your new bride on? Bush greens? Mangoes? Borrowed cassava? Ah! Life had become really hard! And there were these two diseases that were killing people like dogs. This *thin* disease and this stiff-neck disease. Would they ever go away on their own? No! Why? There were too many angry spirits roaming around, spirits that wanted to be propitiated. Look how many people had died since the first fall of Bwete! Could the elders remember all those who were slaughtered like goats when Idi came to power? In barracks? In private houses? What about those ones who thought they were being taken to Tanzania for military training but instead had their heads chopped off at Owiny-ki-Bul near the Uganda-Sudan border? And those who had died in wars that had happened since then? Those whose graves were not known, for whom no burial and funeral rites had been performed? If they had been buried but their spirits still brought disease, drought and famine, their bones would have been dug up and burnt in a swamp! For they would have become *cen*, vengeful spirits, bearers of misfortune. But what could one do now? He, Acuman, would

95

urge the elders to invite the spirits to a feast, and after they had drunk and eaten, chase them into a swamp and leave them there. The spirits would not dare leave the swamp for fear of a second round of banishment. That was the only way to deal with the vengeance spirits, the evil agents that brought suffering and pestilences!

***

The chasing of the evil spirits took a lot of people by surprise. Some fled their homes, thinking that it was the Joseph Kony rebels that had struck, and hid in the bushes until morning. The spirit -chase started in Ayer to the north-east of Teboke and followed the main road to Cegere. As it progressed past Teboke Elementary School, and the top of the road that led to Teboke Catholic mission, few people noticed the resplendent church. The spirits were chased along the murram road with pleas and insults, and with noise from metal containers and calabashes and saucepans and any other noise-making thing that came to hand. The people who took part in the chase – young and old, men and women, adolescent girls and boys, little children – stretched over a distance of three kilometres along the road. As they jogged along they chanted incantations:

Tin omio-wu cam.	Today we have given you food.
Omio-wu cam!	Given you food!
Tin omio-wu mat.	Today we have given you drink.
Omio-wu mat!	Given you drink!
Aman otero-wu paco.	Now we are taking you home.
Otero-wu paco!	Taking you home!
Me pe ikeli-wa wunu two.	So that you do not bring us disease.
Pe ikeli-wa two!	Not bring us disease!
Me kot dwogi.	So that it may rain again.
Kot dwogi!	Rain again!
En olubu ked-wu yoo-ni.	We are taking you along this broad road.
En olubu yoo-ni!	Along this broad road!
Me dere-wa pong.	So that our granaries may be full.
Dere-wa pong!	May be full!

Omito yot kom.	We want health.
Yot kom!	Health!
Omito cam bed tye.	We want food.
Cam bed tye!	Food!
Omito nywalo otino apol.	We want more children.
Otino apol!	More children!

Alongside the pleas insults flew around. Insults directed at the spirits' big and ugly heads, and their short stature; at their abominable eating habits and the filthiness of their living quarters; at their mothers' private parts and old wrinkled breasts...

When the procession reached Ilee swamp, close to Cegere, they left the spirits there. Along with all the things they had used to scare the spirits and make them run. It was already dawn.

Tired, hungry and sleepy-eyed, the spirit-chasers streamed back to their homes, all of them filled with hope.

But the rain did not come. Neither that month nor during the months that followed.

And the *thin* disease did not go away.

And the stiff-neck disease disappeared only for a short while, and then it came back.

Chapter XI

As Adoli-Awal's wife, Pascolina had led a life full of snubs and humiliations. It surprised her that she had not yet greyed, and that she was not even very bitter, despite the doubts and worries that so constantly plagued her.

Thirty-four years ago Adoli-Awal had presented himself in her father's compound and asked for her hand. It had come to her as a complete surprise that a young man such as Adoli-Awal, who had girls buzzing around him all the time like *ojur* insects around a pot of millet beer, should want to marry her. Were not many of those girls of better family than herself? Had they not stayed in school longer than her who had dropped out in Standard Six and then trained as a nursing aide? What was it that Adoli-Awal had seen in her that he could not see in the other girls?

Pascolina's mother, Alimaci, had also asked a lot of questions.

'Pascolina,' she had told her daughter, 'my head is not at peace. Has Adoli-Awal shown any interest in you before?'

'Truly mother,' Pascolina responded, ' he always greets and talks to me whenever he meets me. Mostly about things that are not important. But a number of times he has told me he wanted to marry me. Jokingly. I did not take him seriously.'

'Why does he think you are better than all the girls who are always hovering around him?' Alimaci asked.

'I do not know.'

'My daughter, when he comes here again ask him a lot of questions. Ask him why he does not want to choose a wife from among his many lovers. Ask him why he wants to marry the daughter of an *akopi* whereas he is the son of a county chief. Ask him why a man who has studied at Makerere University should want to marry someone who cannot say anything deep in English. Ask him why.'

That was one of the things that worried Pascolina then – her little education. If she accepted Adoli-Awal's offer of marriage, would he not feel ashamed of her in the presence of his diploma'ed and degreed friends? Especially since his mouth was so full of English so much of the time? Would she not become his village wife while his eyes roamed around for other, better-educated women to marry? Especially in Kampala? She had never been to Kampala, the capital city, though she had heard a lot about it. About how many of the Kampala women painted their lips and fried their hair in order to look beautiful, and about how they dipped themselves in drumfuls of boiling herbs to acquire pink skins so that they could look like white women. She had seen Tabica Akullu who had returned to the village after living in Kampala for ten years. She had been as dark as a moonless night before her departure for Kampala, but when she returned they had gasped in shock. They had mistaken her for a *chatora* – a half-caste – for her skin had become very light; and her once tight, crinkly, jet-black hair had become limp and brown, and so long it fell down to her shoulders.

Pascolina had also heard that the women in Kampala were very wild, that they could snatch your husband while you were looking. And that most of them could speak Luganda, even those of them who were not Baganda. Since Adoli-Awal himself spoke Luganda, having studied for so long in Buganda, how sure could she be that he would not gang up with his Luganda-speaking girlfriends against her? Pascolina thought these thoughts and many other thoughts, but she could not come to the end of them.

What finally decided Pascolina was what she knew people thought about the nursing profession. Most of the men she knew believed that nurses were generally easy, unstable and arrogant women who were not good for marriage. Was it not a common saying that a nurse's eyes were as many as those of a spanner – that their eyes could be interested in many different men at the same time? Nurses were supposed to have been spoilt by rich patients and doctors who frequently gave them money and slept with them. Only a fool would marry a nurse. If someone wanted to marry a career woman, then he should pick a teacher. Teachers had a lot of discipline, they were stable and humble. Pascolina wondered what had earned the nurses that reputation, which she knew was not entirely correct. She knew a large number of loose, unstable teachers, also a lot of decent, disciplined nurses that could make good wives. But Pascolina also knew that when the public chose to believe something, even if it was a myth, they would continue believing it – and very steadfastly too – in spite of evidence to the contrary. She thought about what the locals believed about soldiers: that they were injected with lion's urine to make them fierce and strong. How many lions would they have to kill to obtain so much urine? Or was the urine milked from live lions? Who did the milking and in what quantities? And did becoming a soldier make one's tissues different from those of other people, who would die a slow, painful death if injected with urine, any type of urine at all? But many of the people Pascolina knew would not accept such reasoning. In fact they would not allow you to finish before ordering you to stop questioning the wisdom of those who had seen the soldiers being injected with syringefuls of lion's urine. In short, they would order you to shut up. Had not Paulo Owula and Lacito Ningo broken into a fight over the issue of injectable lion's urine at Abari market and broken a big pot of beer being drunk by several marketgoers, an offence for which they were beaten up by the drinkers and made to pay compensation? As a result, Pascolina concluded that if she did not marry Mike Adoli-Awal, who would marry her? It was better to marry a bad man than to have no husband at all! In any case, you would still have your children to draw consolation from.

Pascolina's mother had not opposed her daughter's decision, but she had not accepted it with enthusiasm either. 'Pascolina,' she had said, 'I do not mind sharing your father with many women, so long as I do not know who I am sharing him with. Also so long as he continues treating me with respect. I know your father, like most men, had a number of affairs before he grew too old to take much interest in women. I would have been surprised if he had not had such affairs since women find him so attractive. I hear he even has a grown-up son with a Muruli woman around Lake Kyoga. But I have had very few problems in my marriage apart from those of poverty and ill-health. I want to give you only one little piece of advice. Even if Adoli-Awal takes a second wife, as long as he continues treating you as his wife, and as long as he does not put her up in your own house, stay put. But the moment he begins treating you badly, or throws you out altogether, come back home. We shall not turn you away.'

Mike Adoli-Awal had married Pascolina and had not taken a second wife. But his forays among the womenfolk, young and old, married and unmarried, had become part of local folklore.

It had all started when she had just got pregnant with their second child, when the first one was one-year-eight-months old. She had not known that her husband possessed such an insatiable thirst for attention until that time. In the presence of women, he renounced all pretence to decorum and behaved like an adolescent, even though he was already a member of parliament, young as he was. At political rallies, at funeral ceremonies, at religious and secular feasts – it was all the same. And if somebody made the mistake of striking up a Lango beer song, Adoli-Awal would dance like someone inhabited by the spirit of a mad man. The first time she had seen him dance to a beer song was at the last funeral rites of one of his constituents. She had watched him silently and shaken her head, wondering what strange spirit had entered him.

It was around 8.00 a.m. The moment the song struck up, Adoli-Awal shot out of his seat beside her, his coattails flying, his shod feet scattering the spear grass that had been laid on the ground to smother the dust in all directions. The other guests seated in the long grass shed erupted into applause.

When Adoli-Awal reached the spot where he intended to dance, he scuffed the ground with the toes of his shoes, then leapt up high, twisting his torso to one side. Then he came back down with a heavy grunt. Hrrm! Then he ran forward a little while stamping his feet, came to a halt and danced at one spot for a few moments, with his arms flailing all around him. That was when the women joined him. They crowded around him and each one of them did a little fast-paced dancing in front of him. Some of the women ululated around him and others whispered things into his ears. And he in turn bent his tall frame and whispered into their ears things that either made them smile wistfully or laugh loudly. Eh-hey! And the eyes of the women's husbands turned red with jealousy. But the women sang on in their thin voices, ululating and eddying around Adoli-Awal like a shoal of fish, their eyes wide and bright.

Yia wang ikomi   I am angry with you

101

Yia wang ikomi	I am angry with you
Omoro wange	You lust after
Ikom meg-ajo.	Other men's wives.
Yia wang ikomi	I am angry with you
Yia wang ikomi	I am angry with you
Omoro wange	You lust after
kom meg-ajo.	Other men's wives.
Inyomo meri ararac	You marry an ugly woman
Inyomo meri ararac	You marry an ugly woman
Ite moro wangi	Then you rivet your eyes
Ikom meg-ajo.	On other men's wives.
Inyomo meri ararac	You marry an ugly woman
Inyomo meri ararac	You marry an ugly woman
Ite moro wangi	Then you rivet your eyes
Ikom meg-ajo.	On other's men's wives.

And the Honourable Adoli-Awal leapt up and landed, raising a big cloud of dust. Then he shaped his hands into a horn and blew into them. Too-loo! Too-loo! Too-loo! And did not pay any attention to Pascolina, his wife, at all.

Whenever Adoli-Awal was, there was *lelo*, happiness!

Then President Bwete had fallen from power for the first time and Mike Adoli-Awal had had to go into a six-year exile sometime after that. He had gone into exile alone leaving Pascolina behind. After his return from exile, Pascolina thought that the sufferings of exile and Adoli-Awal's relative maturity should have reformed him. A few years later, however, she was to hear a scandalous story about him and his exploits in Zambia. It was when Adoli-Awal was a member of the Broadbased National Assembly and a junior Minister in Uchebi's government when this happened. Bwete had fallen again and General Ragamoi, who had supplanted Bwete, had in his turn fled the country.

Adoli-Awal had travelled to Lusaka, Zambia, with some of his fellow members of the Broadbased National Assembly and booked into a hotel that fitted his status. They were meant to stay in Zambia for a week, studying how the Zambian tax regime worked. The first two days went by without trouble. On the third day, however, Adoli-Awal started taking a more than normal interest in one of the hotel cleaners, one of those who cleaned and polished the rooms on his floor, Floor 3. Every morning at around 10.00 a.m. the cleaner would rap on the room doors and announce: 'Housekeeping! Housekeeping! Housekeeping!' Now it happened that Miss Housekeeping had the kind of figure that Adoli-Awal craved – tall, plumpish, with a wasp-waist. She also had a fascinating face – long, narrow and tapering towards the chin, with narrow, dreamy, lynx-like eyes. And she spoke English in a slow, soft, lilting way.

It was on the fourth day, three days before he was due to travel back to Uganda, that Adoli-Awal first did something about Miss Housekeeping. When she came shouting 'Housekeeping! Housekeeping!' at 10.30 a.m. on that fourth day, Adoli-Awal was still in bed, with his rich Raymonds blanket drawn up to his square chin. The moment Miss Housekeeping rapped on his door and announced 'Housekeeping! Housekeeping!' he leapt up, wrapped a monogrammed hotel towel around his waist and opened the door. He then invited Miss Housekeeping to come inside and sit next to him on the bed.

'Sit beside you, sir? What for?' she asked, wariness creeping into her dreamy eyes. She did not budge from the corridor. He went back to the bed and sat on it.

'First come sit next to me here and I will tell you,' he answered, while thumping a spot beside him with his fist. Miss Housekeeping did not move. Adoli-Awal rubbed his hands together, cocked his head and eyed Miss Housekeeping the way a kite would eye a chick. 'Standing around in the corridor won't help you much,' he addressed Miss Housekeeping through the open door.

'Sir,' Miss Housekeeping pleaded, ' I have work to do, and I cannot do it with you inside the room.'

Adoli-Awal cleared his throat, leaned over and picked up his brown, leather-bound diary off the top of his bedside table. Miss Housekeeping looked at the diary curiously, craning her long neck into the room from the safety of her corridor. As Adoli-Awal opened the diary a flurry of US dollar bills fluttered to the floor. He picked them up one by one and put them back among the pages of the diary. 'Can't you come inside and take a closer look at this?' Adoli-Awal urged as he waved the dollared diary about.

'Not if you are still inside that room!' Miss Housekeeping purred and her head vanished. A few seconds later Adoli-Awal heard her hard-soled shoes tap-tapping away down the corridor.

The next day – the fifth day – Adoli-Awal waited for Miss Housekeeping, but instead of her soft, lilting voice he heard the gruff, deep voice of a man. In disgust, Adoli-Awal got up and shuffled off to the bathroom to brush his teeth and to shower. He left the room soon after.

It was on the sixth day, a day prior to his scheduled departure, that Miss Housekeeping showed up again. This time she did not come announcing 'Housekeeping! Housekeeping!' She instead sneaked up to his door and tapped on it lightly.

'Who's that?' he asked, his voice gruff with irritation. She did not answer but knocked again, harder, beating a rapid tattoo on the door.

Adoli-Awal got up off the bed, muttering something about people who thought they had the right to disturb other people's sleep. He wrapped a hotel towel around his waist and approached the door. A flurry of raps assaulted the door.

Adoli-Awal inserted the key in the key hole, turned it. Then he jerked the door open. Only to be confronted by Miss Housekeeping standing in the corridor, a broom in one hand and a bucket in the other.

'Oh sorry,' he spluttered.

Miss Housekeeping grinned.

'Come in,' he invited.

She came into the room carrying the broom and bucket with her.

After a very short negotiation, Adoli-Awal and Miss Housekeeping struck up a deal. She settled for thirty US dollars, cash before delivery. She deposited the three ten-dollar bills Adoli gave her in a pocket sown inside the left cup of her bra. She then got into Adoli-Awal's bed, uniform and all, and invited Adoli-Awal to join her.

'Brazen bitch,' Adoli-Awal thought. 'Day before yesterday she was pretending to be a virgin. Now look what she is doing.' Then he got under the blanket and lay next to her.

104

The fun had not even begun yet when Adoli-Awal noticed that the door to his room was wide open and the figure of a tall, burly security man filled it.

'This man is raping me, come and help!' Miss Housekeeping shrieked to Security, who slipped into the room, locked the door unhurriedly behind him and ambled towards the bed.

Adoli-Awal's vision exploded into a fireworks of strong, blinding colours. When it cleared, Security stood, strong and solid like a wardrobe over him, asking him contemptuously why he had decided to rape a member of the hotel staff.

Adoli-Awal had to put up with two blinding slaps and part with 600 US dollars before Security could let him be. The moment Security received the money, Miss Housekeeping, who had been sitting forlorn and dejected on the edge of his bed, shot up, picked up her bucket and broom and fled the room. Security followed suit, carefully closing the door with a soft click.

It made Adoli-Awal feel sick to realise that he had been set up. He returned from Zambia a very subdued man.

Pascolina had been twenty-three when she got married. She had been a fairly tall, small-boned woman with very dark skin, broad hips, slender feet and wide, laughing eyes then. Now in her fifties, the last few years of good feeding and inactivity, along with her age, had turned her into a large, flabby woman without a recognisable waist. The most remarkable thing about the mature Pascolina was, however, her eyes. They had lost the humorous sparkle of her youth and taken on a cold, reptilian watchfulness. That, along with the tight grimness around her mouth, frightened a lot of people.

***

It was April. The Honourable Adoli-Awal had been away in Kampala for six months when he first heard about it. He had been away debating important things at the Broadbased National Assembly and, as a junior Minister, attending to important matters of state.

The bringer of the bad news was none other than Adoli-Awal's wife, Pascolina.

The news that Pascolina brought her husband from Teboke that April had to do with what Abudu Olwit, the officer in charge of

105

Alaro Prison Farm, was doing for Teboke and some of the neighbouring villages. And Mike Adoli-Awal found the news worrying.

'Go home now and see with your own eyes,' Pascolina told her husband. 'Borehole pumps are being set up everywhere in Teboke, Alaro, Ayer and Abolo. Abudu Olwit has brought some white men who seem only too willing to do his bidding. Now everyone is full of praise for him and his mother. They no longer treat her with as much contempt as they used to. If you do not watch out you might not have a seat in parliament next time. Olwit is becoming too popular.'

'When did all this begin?' Adoli-Awal enquired.

'About two months ago. And the machines that sink the boreholes are fast. They are not the type that takes a month or more pounding a hole into the ground. These ones just cut holes into the ground. Very fast. It takes only two or three days for a borehole to be sunk and cemented. Let me tell you, there are boreholes everywhere in your constituency now.'

Mike Adoli-Awal suspected Pascolina was exaggerating about boreholes being 'everywhere' in his constituency, but still the news was nothing short of alarming. He had heard about the drought that had afflicted a large part of his constituency but he had felt powerless to do anything about it apart from asking for food aid. No-one had, however, taken his request seriously. If it had been a district, he was told, something would have been done about the situation. But a constituency was a small thing about which he was not expected to bother a lot of important people. In any case, food could be bought from the neighbouring constituencies and distributed to the inhabitants of the drought-stricken area. Did he need the government to do that for him? Couldn't he channel his request to some of these organisations that dealt with such problems as famine and see if they could help? Feeling depressed and utterly helpless, he had decided to keep away from his constituency until the situation improved, instead of having to contend with his constituents' questions about why he was not helping them with their problems.

And now Abudu Olwit had sneaked in and filled his place.

Four months into the drought, which had ended up lasting for eight months, a delegation of Olwit's mother's relatives and other

106

people had come to see Olwit at Alaro Prison Farm. The delegation included Olwit's maternal uncle, Odwong. They told him about how, though his father, being a Mugisu, was alien, he, Olwit, was still one of them, for Alicinora's blood flowed in his body, and that blood was also theirs. Had it not been said that it was always only one's mother who stayed around to wipe one's tears and nose when one's father was away chasing after other women? And that you could not point with confidence at the man who married your mother and say 'That is my father'? What if it turned out that your real father was the notorious chicken or goat thief, or even night dancer? How people who knew you would laugh at your silly assertion about your mother's husband being your father, behind your back! But the person who gave birth to you could not be anything but your mother, and her clan cold not be anything but your clan too!

'Our son,' a member of the delegation told him, 'suffering does not belong to any one person. Suffering belongs to us all. Today, suffering may visit my home and tomorrow, it may be your turn. You have not been to see us since you were posted to Alaro Prison Farm. The only people you visit are your mother and your uncle Odwong here. Yet we are also your people. We belong together. What affects us also affects your uncle, and your mother.

'This drought has visited us and refused to go away. The soil just burns up the crops and there is no water in the wells and dams. Our cows and goats are hungry and thin and few people want to buy them in the markets of Aduku, Minakulu and Otwal. Like us, the animals are dying a slow death that may leave our villages only for the crows and vultures to roam around in.

'Our son, you know people both here and elsewhere. Try to talk to them. They may be ready to help us. Hunger is very painful, our son. We want something to eat.'

There was so much pain and despair on the haggard faces of the delegation. That alone touched his heart. They really did not need to tell him about their predicament.

Abudu Olwit suspected that many members of the delegation were feeling guilty about not having been close to him before, about having not even attempted to be close. So it was possible they thought he would not be willing to listen to them. That was probably the reason why they had brought his uncle Odwong along. Odwong had a lot of leverage with him, and he considered him more of a parent than his mother, Alicinora. For if it had not been for Odwong, who had sacrificed so much to ensure that he received an education, where would he be now? Without Odwong's dedication and constant encouragement, would he not have ended up like so many of his former schoolmates who now treated him with so much embarrassing deference and fawning? Who sometimes crawled up to him to beg him to buy them a cigarette or two, or one inkpotful of *arege*?

It made Abdu Olwit feel good, and at the same time it hurt him, to know that now his mother's people wanted to take him into their clan. The clan wanted to take him in, it was holding out both its arms to him. He would walk into those arms and see how warm the embrace was, how long it would last. If he did not find enough warmth within the embrace, if he sensed only cold and calculating trickery, he could always pull back. For did it not happen that the closest of siblings and the most intimate of couples sometimes parted company – and often permanently too – over something quite trivial? Well, he, Olwit, would try to belong somewhere at least, or be seen to belong somewhere. He was tired of being an outsider. He did not belong with his mother as an individual. She seemed to be particularly determined never to be a real part of him right from the moment he was born, from the moment the birth attendant, Akaci, had cut the umbilical cord that had stoutly linked him to her. She had fed him and allowed him to grow bodily up. But she had not nourished him in any other way. Her instructions to him had mostly come in the form of insults and screams, and her admonitions and reprimands in the form of humiliating snubs and putdowns. Abudu Olwit sometimes wondered why his mother had not strangled him at birth or during early childhood since he seemed to be only a source of pain to her instead of being a source of joy. Yet, strangely, though he did not have much affection for her, he did not harbour any hatred against her either. He pitied her, but was also a little frightened of her. Did other people feel the same way about their mothers too? Olwit wondered.

A month before the visit by the delegation from his mother's clan, an NGO had come to Alaro Prison Farm to set up borehole pumps and advise on irrigation. It was a Scandinavian NGO called

IRDSA, International Relief for Disaster-Struck Areas. Its major role was to help establish infrastructure meant to ensure that the areas that received their help could avoid disasters such as famine in a more sustainable manner. They would provide funds, equipment and technical advice, but would mostly employ local people so as to provide jobs and impart skills. After working at Alaro Prison Farm for seven weeks, IRDSA had proceeded to Kotido district in the north-east of the country.

Abudu Olwit felt that the best way in which to help 'his' people was not to give them handouts of food. Securing food for distribution to them would only be a stop-gap measure. Of course the people would need something to eat that was more substantial than the wild greens and mangoes that were available to them at that moment. More nutritious food would ensure that they had the strength to work their fields when the rains returned after the long drought.

Abudu Olwit personally travelled to Kotido to request IRDSA for help. They asked him to write a project proposal. When he returned to Alaro Prison Farm he put together a team of four young men to do this job, and they came up with a project proposal within ten days. He sent the proposal by courier to IRDSA and their response was positive.

When the Honourable Adoli-Awal's wife told him about the boreholes, the last borehole pump was being installed. Total: Six borehole pumps in his constituency. At last the locals did not have to walk or ride miles to Okole swamp to fetch water.

When Adoli-Awal arrived in Teboke – together with his wife – IRDSA had embarked on another project. It was a week after she had gone to see him in Kampala. They had started digging two new cattle dams, one in Teboke and the second one in Alemi, five miles to the northeast of Teboke. Adoli-Awal also heard that Abudu Olwit had become a frequent presence at burials, funerals and feasts, where he was expected to bring – and did bring – water in the big tractor-towed water tank belonging to Alaro Prison Farm. And he often also ferried loads of firewood by tractor to such occasions.

Chapter XII

When you walk down the main street of Teboke trading centre you will not miss it. Start your stroll from the northern end of the trading centre, where the murram road from Corner Loro joins the one from Corner Ayer and they become one, like two tributaries emptying into a river. Where the two roads join, to your right as you face down the main street is what used to be a laterite quarry, a deep and large pit from which Public Works Department tipper trucks used to obtain murram to build and repair roads. People call the large pit *pidawulidi*, a corruption of PWD, Public Works Department. The quarry is now overgrown with grass and tall *abwori* plants, but it is still deep enough to hurt someone who falls into it, and it might easily harbour snakes. Take a leisurely walk past the quarry while looking to your right. A short distance beyond the quarry you will find yourself at the upper end of a broad, tree-bordered murram drive that sweeps away towards a grove of old eucalyptus trees, trees old enough to be grown-up men with children. These trees stand behind, and tower above, a splendorous round church with a high, spiked roof of strong, red *mabati*. The walls of the church are stout and ribbed, and are finished with maroon roughcast. Stained-glass windows puncture the upper reaches of the church and cast a soft, mysterious spell inside the church. The church and the eucalyptus trees are all part of Teboke Catholic mission.

You might want to take a peep inside the church.

Or you might even want to kneel down and pray to the image of the Virgin Mary, or to that of Jesus Christ on the Cross.

Or you might instead prefer to walk right past the top of the church drive and start off down the main street of Teboke trading centre.

Well, that is your choice.

The moment you start walking down the main street, look only to your left. And count the buildings. The tenth building, an old building with walls of sun-baked bricks plastered with sand mixed with *arege* residue, and crowned with a flat roof of rusty *mabati* that slopes down from front to back, is Namu's bar-restaurant. It has a large sign painted in stylised letters on old, rough timber that reads:

Namu's BaR & ResTuaraNT
You can Eat & Drink
HERE

The sign, which reposes on sledge-like feet, is kept inside the bar when the bar goes to sleep. Then at daybreak it is carried out and placed at the side of the road so that it can beckon passers-by into the bar-restaurant.

The man who painted the sign, a Senior Three dropout with a lot of artistic talent, is called Geoffrey Olike. At first he had written:

Namu's BaR & ResTauraNT

But his friend, Kassim Opido, who claimed to have excelled in French in secondary school, emphatically told him that 'restaurant' was French, that the English equivalent was 'restuarant', spelt with the 'a' coming after the 'u', not before it. Geoffrey Olike, like the good listener he was, had followed his friend's advice and dutifully changed 'au' to 'ua', so that the sign now read:

Namu's BaR & ResTuaRaNT

Three weeks after the sign had been written, a young man, Francis Olam, a caterer trained at Topcare School of Catering and Accountancy in Kampala, approached Geoffrey Olike and told him that 'restuarant' was the wrong spelling. Having trained as a caterer, he said, he knew lots of words, many of them of French origin, related to the hospitality industry. Now 'restaurant' was the correct spelling in both English and French, he added. Olike told Olam that he had done what he had been hired by the bar-restaurant owner to do, namely, to paint a sign as beautifully as he could. If one or two words were incorrectly spelt, that was none of his business. After all many of the people who passed by the sign every day possessed only a scanty knowledge of English, or were not even able to read at all, in any language known to man. The sign was not all that important anyway since anyone with a grain of intelligence could get a clue about what went on in the place from the way the place looked. In

111

any case he was not going to spend the rest of his life painting and repainting one English word.

Irene Namu was very popular with the men of Teboke and the neighbouring villages. Most of the married women, especially the younger ones, however, resented, even loathed, her. For when the men went into Namu's bar-restaurant, there was no knowing what they would do in there. Certainly they drank. But frequently they also ate there, and very heavily too. Too heavily to want to eat when they staggered back home at night, their breaths foul and pungent with drink. When their wives asked them why they did not want to eat, the men would frequently plead an aching stomach or a throbbing headache. The moment they got into bed, however, they would sink into a deep, contented and untroubled sleep, as if the contact with the bed had instantly got rid of the bellyache and headache. And often after getting up in the morning they promptly asked for something fatty to eat with a lot of pepper and onion! The women knew that all this was Irene Namu's doing!

Sometimes, however, the men's luck ran out. Like the day Jasper Munu was caught munching away on cock-back.

Jasper Munu had left home at 10:00 a.m. that Saturday and strolled down to the trading centre, where he had bought some millet beer at *Imat* Kulu's place and started drinking it with friends. Shortly afterwards, however, Munu's eldest daughter, Apici, aged ten, had come looking for Munu. She had informed him that her baby sister, Akoli, had become fire-hot all over and was shivering very badly. Her mother wanted to take the child to Patrick Luru's clinic nearby but had no money. She had therefore been sent to ask him for money.

'Apici,' Jasper Munu told his daughter firmly, 'when I come away to drink I do not want to be disturbed. If I wanted you to keep disturbing me with your endless requests, I would not be here right now. I would still be sitting around at home. Tell your mother that I do not have any money, that even this beer that I am drinking, I am drinking it on credit. Do you hear?'

'But mother said that if I do not get any money from you, I should not go back home.'

112

'Apici, what has happened to your ears? Has somebody pushed gum into them?' Munu screamed, feigning anger. 'I am saying that I do not have any money right now. Have you now understood?'

'Yes *Apap*,' Apici replied. Then she shambled away, downcast.

Jasper Munu went back to his drinking.

Now it seemed that the baby's condition had got really bad. Or it could be that Apici's mother was angered by her husband's response beyond the point of tolerance. But still she was patient enough to cook a lunch of mashed cassava and *bojo* greens for her family. Then she flung the baby onto her back and strapped her with an old towel before storming *Imat* Kulu's place.

She did not find Munu there.

And the men who were still drinking there told her that they did not know where Munu had proceeded to.

And as she tramped around the trading centre looking for her husband, her inside flamed with anger.

After a long search, Apici's mother found her husband hunkered down on a cane stool behind Namu's bar-restaurant, eating the roasted back of a big cock.

Now it happens that in Teboke when a chicken is being cut up for barbecuing, the neck is considered to be part of the back. So the person who buys a chicken back can work his way from the tip of the neck through to the raised fatty tail-tip. Munu's cock-back had been smeared with curry powder together with onion and red pepper and then roasted. The moment he had bought the cock-back he had immediately twisted off the fleshy tail-tip and dropped it into his mouth, rolling it around and savouring the hot spiciness of the fatty morsel. He had swallowed the tail-tip and held the cock-back up, at first undecided about which part of the cock-back to tackle next. Then he had snapped off a piece of the neck, dropped it into his mouth and chewed it slowly, crushing the sweet marrow-filled bones with his strong, white teeth. He had swallowed that morsel too, and then had decided that biting off pieces of cock-back was more enjoyable than breaking or tearing them off. So he had bitten into the remainder of the chicken neck and started worrying it, twisting his head to left and right like a dog worrying a bone.

113

It was at that moment that Munu's wife appeared, carrying their baby strapped to her work-stiffened back. She approached Munu from behind. Munu was too preoccupied with his cock-back to hear her footsteps at first. When he finally heard them, she was almost upon him . He did not know what to do with the cock-back.

'Munu,' she called, her voice low and cold as the dry-season morning chill. 'So this is what you hurried away from home for.' It was a statement, not a question.

Munu shifted the cock-back from his right hand to his left. He cleared his throat. He opened his mouth, closed it. He had lost his voice. He went on sitting on the stool, his back still turned to his wife.

'Munu,' his wife spoke, 'if you are not ashamed of what you have been doing, turn round and face me. And tell me that it is all right for a man to refuse to buy medicine for his sick child and instead buy himself roast chicken to eat in hiding. Tell me if that is what your mother taught you about looking after your family.'

Munu's wife stood with her arms behind her back, her hands cradling the buttocks of the baby. The baby stirred and whined. It was breathing with its whole body, heaving and subsiding like a toad.

Munu still held what was left of the cock-back in his left hand. Limply. He stood up slowly, then turned to face his wife.

'Min Apici,' he said. He always addressed her as 'Min Apici', 'Mother of Apici', their first-born daughter. 'Min Apici, no self-respecting woman would be tramping around the trading centre dressed the way you are. Even if she has a sick child.'

Min Apici's green-and-white print dress was mottled with days-old dirt. A tear ran down the skirt of the dress, from around her hip to the hem. Beneath the tear was a half-slip that originally was yellow but that had become brownish through age and washing with insufficient soap. There was another tear in the bodice through which the wrinkled nipple of her left breast showed.

Min Apici glanced down at her dress. Then she spoke.

'Munu,' she said, 'you are my husband. When I wear dirty and ragged clothes, people will not say we saw Min Apici dragging herself around in soiled clothes, but they will say we saw Munu's wife. So my clothes do not shame me, they shame you!'

114

Munu yawned. He lifted his face up and yawned very wide and loud. Aoouw! With the cock-back still in his left hand.

'Min Apici,' he said, 'I thought you had more wisdom than you actually have. If you possessed any wisdom at all you would not be standing around here telling me about your torn and dirty clothes instead of going back home and waiting for me there.'

Min Apici's eyes narrowed with scorn.

'If that is the sort of thing a piece of roast chicken can make you say, then I pity you,' she remarked, and then she looked him up and down. 'Well, I am going back home.' She started loosening the towel with which she had harnessed the child to her back. 'And I am leaving the baby here, so that you can feed it on roast chicken too.'

She slipped the child off her back and dumped it on the ground. The towel fell away from the baby's body. The baby was naked. It shrieked in protest.

Min Apici turned and began to walk away.

'Min Apici,' Munu addressed her back, 'if you think that abandoning your child here is going to help you in any way, you are a fool. Just come back and pick up your child.'

Min Apici stopped and turned.

'Munu,' she said, 'that child is not mine alone. We made her together. If she dies it will not be my loss alone, but yours too.' Then she turned her back and went on her way.

'The stupid woman thinks I care,' Munu muttered. 'I will see if she does not come back.'

The baby heaved and subsided like a toad.

The baby moaned.

The baby shrieked.

But still *Min* Apici did not come back.

Munu could not go back to eating his cock-back. He had lost all appetite for it. He flung the cock-back towards a family of ducks squawking nearby. One of them snatched it up and tried to flee. The others gave chase.

The baby started crawling slowly towards Munu on all fours, leaving the old, soiled towel behind. Gazing at him with glazed, piteous eyes. Heaving and subsiding like a toad. And groaning.

But *Min* Apici was not yet back.

Munu got up and picked up the baby. He flung the baby over his shoulder. The heat from the baby's body burnt his shoulder. Munu hurriedly picked up the towel lying on the ground and flung it around his neck. Then he tramped out of the backyard of Namu's bar-restaurant.

The people of Teboke still talk about the hot fight that Munu and *Min* Apici fought when he arrived back home, carrying his baby daughter on his right shoulder like a small bag of millet grain.

***

Irene Namu's bar-restaurant had grown slowly, without haste. At first serving only a limited variety of beverages, mainly *arege, kwete, wiri* and tea, the bar-restaurant had expanded. Now it also served European liquors, bottled beer and soft drinks. The ugly outside of the building – the roughly plastered walls, the rusting *mabati* roof – concealed much beauty within it. For one, on the inside the walls were painted a soothing light-blue, and repainted whenever they acquired any discernible hint of dirt. There were also lots of pictures on these walls, most of them cut out of western magazines and African newspapers. From the magazines mostly came colour pictures of semi-nude white women walking with their thin hips exaggeratedly swung to left or right, or with their bodies contorted in all sorts of shapes intended to be seductive. Women who seemed to have eaten a proper meal many seasons ago. The newspapers, on the other hand, mostly supplied black-and-white pictures of important political and religious figures, and popular sports personalities. The former fatly smiling down at the drinkers from their lofty perches on the walls, and the latter often tautly launched in one kind of bodily motion or another. The chairs and tables were beautiful too, blue or white plastic furniture bought in Lira town and transported to Teboke in pick-up trucks. The long, curved counter was set up against the wall to your right as you entered the bar-restaurant. The liquors and bottled beer were ranged in the shelves behind the bar counter, whereas the *kwete* and *wiri* were stored in large plastic drums beneath the bank of shelves and scooped up into plastic cups for the drinkers. Being the tough, no-nonsense woman she was, Irene Namu did not allow anyone to drink at the counter, not even her lovers. Everyone had to sit at the tables – inside the bar itself or outside on the verandah, depending on one's preference.

Like the drinks, the menu had also been quite limited at the beginning, mostly roast chicken, which was often eaten alone, and stewed beef which one ate with boiled cassava. Slowly the menu had expanded to include such dishes as goat, duck, grams, cowpeas and pigeon peas. One could eat these with millet *ugali*, mashed cassava, rice or posho. Conspicuously absent was bean stew. Bean stew was deemed to be a poor man's dish and therefore no-one would have wanted to be seen eating it at Namu's bar-restaurant. The general attitude was that if one wanted to eat beans, one had better eat them in one's own home.

Apart from the food and drinks, one of the attractions of Namu's bar-restaurant was Namu herself. She was widely known for her inability to say no to a man – so long as he had some little class and the right kind of money. Her helpers in the bar-restaurant, three local young women called Olympia, Keren and Aguret, seemed to have caught her attitude like an infection. But these helpers went for a lot less. A little drink here, a little food there and they were yours for the evening, or for the whole night.

Namu's bar-restaurant was a very popular place indeed.

Abudu Olwit was one of the patrons of Namu's bar-restaurant. He was frequently to be seen lounging inside the bar-restaurant or outside on the verandah. If the Loro-Teboke road was not flooded along the Okole swamp stretch, he would come in his pick-up. If it was flooded, he would drive one of the powerful Massey Ferguson tractors, especially the four-wheel-drive one.

Usually when he came to drink at Namu's, he would return to Alaro between 10:00 p.m. and 11:00 p.m.

Chapter XIII

'He is a rebel,' the Honourable Adoli-Awal said.

'I am surprised,' the Intelligence Officer responded.

'He is a rebel,' Adoli-Awal repeated, 'and he needs to be watched. Or even arrested outright.'

'From what you say,' the Intelligence Officer remarked, 'he has been enticing people to go to the bush using Alaro Prison Farm facilities and food, right?'

'That's right,' Adoli-Awal affirmed.

The Intelligence Officer jotted something down on a notepad. When he finished he raised his head and looked into Adoli-Awal's eyes. Adoli-Awal gazed right back.

'I hope,' the Intelligence Officer remarked , 'that you are aware of the gravity of this allegation. To allege that somebody is a rebel is something very serious indeed, you know.'

'I am aware,' Adoli-Awal answered. 'And I stand by my word.'

The Honourable Adoli-Awal had gone to see the county Intelligence Officer three days after his arrival home from Kampala. He had not liked what he saw. And what he heard people saying about Abudu Olwit. And about himself.

There were three brand-new borehole water-pumps in Teboke alone. All-steel water-pumps that gleamed in the sunshine and around which people now gathered to fill their containers, to wash their clothes, to wash themselves. And to gossip.

The work at the dam sites in Teboke and Alemi was going on apace. Every day a large crowd assembled at each of the sites to watch the work going on there and to give a hand whenever their labour was required.

Only one marriage had taken place in Teboke during the eight months that the Honourable Adoli-Awal had been away in Kampala, eight months marked by drought, famine and need. And there had occurred many deaths. And Abudu Olwit had been around to console and help the bereaved at the burials of many of those who had died.

Atin-anam was good, the locals said. Look what he had done for them, even though his father was a Mugisu – if he was really the father in the first place – and his mother an *alaya*, a woman of loose morals. He had not had an easy time growing up, they said, what with his mother sleeping around all the time, neglecting him, insulting him, beating him, humiliating him! What with his agemates abusing him, taunting him, humiliating him, ridiculing him, putting him down.

Atin luk!	Bastard child!
Atin anam!	Foreigner's child!
Papi pe!	You have no father!
Jin kong papi nga?	By the way, who is your father?
Atin amero!	A drunkard's child!
Gi a totti oket!	Your mother's thing is tattered (with overuse)!

But *atin-anam* had put aside all the hurts he had suffered and done only good things for them. May God preserve his life!

The Honourable Adoli-Awal began visiting the homes of people he had not deigned to visit before.

***

'I hear that some people are deceiving you that they can be better members of parliament than myself.'

'A-aaa! We have not heard anything yet. No-one has come here to campaign yet.'

'No, I am not talking about people who have come to campaign. I am talking about Olwit and his doings.'

'But he is only helping us.'

'I hear he wants to stand against me.'

'Maybe. But he has not yet told us anything.'

***

'This boy without a father. Do you not think he is wasting his time? This money he is wasting trying to convince people that he can also stand, why does he not build a decent house for himself with it, for instance?'

119

'But has he said he wants to stand for parliament?'

'I have been told he wants to fell me.'

'Well, I have not yet heard that.'

'Fine. You wait and see. Stronger people have tried to fell me but they have failed. What has defeated the axe the hoe cannot cut.'

***

And some people laughed behind Adoli-Awal's back.

Ha...ha...ha...ha! What Olwit is doing has turned Adoli-Awal's stomach into water!

Eh-hey! Fear is really shaking the legs of his trousers!

Ha...ha...ha...ha! If he thinks that he owns us, then he is stupid. His head is rotten.

Yes, his head is sick. Eh-hey!

Eh-hey! Do not kill me with laughter!

The Honourable Adoli-Awal stayed in Teboke for one week, then he went back to his Kampala.

***

Abudu Olwit's arrest came exactly two weeks after Adoli-Awal's return to Kampala. It took place at Namu's bar-restaurant at 8:35 p.m. It was carried out by four men in civilian clothes who burst into the bar-restaurant wielding AK47s and automatic pistols. They ordered everyone to put up their hands and not to move, and commanded Olwit to stand up and come forward with his hands raised. They then pushed Olwit into a Hyundai saloon car and sped off. Stunned, Olwit's fellow patrons sat around for some time after Olwit had been spirited away, talking in low voices among themselves. Then they started drifting away into the night. Twenty minutes later not a single soul was left in Namu's bar-restaurant.

The news of Abudu Olwit's arrest reached both his mother-in-law, Bitoroci, and his mother, Alicinora, that same night. The first to hear about it was Bitoroci, who was kneading millet bread in a saucepan over a three-stone fireplace in her detached kitchen, all the while chattering away with her three-year-old granddaughter, Lilly.

120

'*Atat,* what are we going to eat with the millet bread? White-ant paste?'

Bitoroci laughs, then answers: 'No, my grandchild . White-ant paste is not nice with millet bread.'

'What is nice with millet bread then?'

'Chicken.'

'Fried chicken?'

'Yes.'

'Also chicken cooked with groundnut paste?'

'Yes.'

'Also beef?'

'Yes.'

'Also goat's meat?'

'Yes.'

'Also eggplant?'

'I like it. It is nice.'

'I hate it.'

'*Atat*?'

'Yes?'

'*Kodi,*' a call came from the doorway of the kitchen.

'*Karibu,*' Bitoroci answered.

'Can I come in?' the man's voice said.

'Enter,' Bitoroci said.

The man entered. It was Kalvin Pule, the young man who barbecued beef and goat's meat at Namu's bar-restaurant.

Bitoroci cast her eyes around the kitchen for a chair or stool but could see none. Pule understood what her looking around meant. She was looking for something to give him to sit on.

Pule cleared his throat. 'I have not come here to sit,' he said. 'I have brought some news. Bad news.'

Bitoroci's hands abandoned the long, thin kneading stick and she jerked around to squarely face Pule.

'Do not tell me that somebody has died,' she said, her voice shrill with panic.

'No,' Pule said. 'I was at Namu's place this evening. Working. It was already dark. Some four men drove up to the place in a white

121

car and got out. They were all carrying guns. Machine guns. They ordered everyone in the bar to lie down on the floor and dragged your son-in-law Olwit into their car. They have taken him away.'

'What are you saying?' she asked, her voice a strangled whine.

'I am saying that Olwit has been taken away by some strange men.'

'Oh my people,' she exclaimed, 'we are all dead!'

Pule still stood around inside the small kitchen, not knowing what to do next.

'*Atat,*' Lilly called.

'Wait a moment,' Bitoroci replied, a little gruffly. She drew herself up, slowly, to her full height. She had stripped the *ikoyi* she wore down to her waist because of the heat. Now she dragged it up to cover her long, broad, hanging breasts and knotted it over her breastbone. She started out of the kitchen. Pule stepped out of her way.

'*Atat,*' Lilly called, 'where are you going?'

'Oh,' Bitoroci said, 'I had forgotten that you were there. Come!'

Lilly walked over to her grandmother, who took her small hand into hers. They stepped out into the darkness outside together. They went into the main house.

Kalvin Pule left the kitchen and walked off to look for *arege* to drink for the night.

In the main house Bitoroci snapped up a large cloth, lifted Lilly up and flung her onto her back, harnessing her tightly with the cloth. Then she dashed out of the house and ran off towards Alicinora's home, beating her breast with both her hands as she trotted along, chanting:

> *Aido! Aido!* Olwit is dead!
> *Aido! Aido!* Olwit is dead!
> *Aido! Aido!* Olwit is dead!
> *Aido! Aido!* Olwit is dead!

She went on chanting until she reached Alicinora's home. The door to Alicinora's sleeping hut was half-open.

When Bitoroci went in she found Alicinora lying across her grass-filled cotton mattress laid on a reed bed. Her feet were resting on the floor. She was lying dishevelled on her back with her mouth wide open, and snoring like a pregnant pig. Riiit ... tirrrr ... riiit ... tirrrr ... riiit ... tirrrr ... Bitoroci knew that Alicinora should have been sleeping on a better mattress. Her son Olwit had twice bought her a six-inch Vitafoam mattress, but each time she had sold it off in order to be able to afford the large quantities of *arege* that she drank. Abudu Olwit had refused to buy her a third mattress in order to teach her a lesson.

It took Bitoroci the better part of ten minutes to wake Alicinora up.

On waking up Alicinora slipped off the bed and fell in a heap on the floor. Then she slowly lifted herself on her elbows and sat up.

'Who is this?' she asked drunkenly.

'*Dyera*,' Bitoroci said, 'I am the one.'

'Who? Bitoroci?' she asked, and then she yawned long and wide. Aooouw!

'*Dyera*,' Bitoroci pleaded, 'listen.'

'First sit down,' Alicinora slurred, 'I came back with some *arege*. My son has married into your family. I would not want you to go back to your home with your stomach empty. We shall drink the *arege* as we talk.'

'We can drink that *arege* tomorrow,' Bitoroci said firmly, getting impatient. 'For the moment, *you* listen.'

'Well, I am listening.'

Then Bitoroci told Alicinora about four tall men who came to Namu's bar-restaurant that night. They were carrying guns such as were used by soldiers, as well as big clubs. They charged into Namu's bar-restaurant and asked, 'Which of you is Olwit?' and Olwit dropped and took cover under the table at which he had been drinking. The four men ordered everybody in the bar to stay put or they would get blown up. Then two of them went to where Olwit was cowering under the table and dragged him out. Even before they reached the verandah of the bar-restaurant, they had already started kicking, slapping and clubbing him. Now those who had always envied her because of her daughter's marriage to Olwit were happy because Olwit was dead!

123

By the time Bitoroci and Alicinora reached Eripadica's home in Alee village, three miles to the east of Teboke, Alicinora had sobered up a great deal.

Eripadica was widely known for her gift with herbs. She had cured many people of *amot*, the affliction that broke people's backs, and *ikodo*, the disease that ate away one's nose. Eripadica was also known for being a very good spirit medium. She could speak to the dead as easily as other people spoke to the living. Was she not the one who had summoned the spirit of Ojuka, the Uganda Army corporal who had been killed in the Masaka army barracks by Idi's soldiers, so that Ojuka's mother could learn how her son had died? And had people not heard how Ojuka had pleaded with his killers to spare his life, how he had wept, how he had gurgled when his neck was being cut? That she was a very good spirit medium was in no doubt at all.

People did not have reservations about Eripadica's powers of divination either. She had, for example, helped many women retrieve their fertility, the most remarkable case being *Min* Ogwal's. *Min* Ogwal - 'Mother of Ogwal' - had given birth to only one child, a boy called Ogwal, and had promptly become barren. *Min* Ogwal had visited many medicine men and medicine women, she had visited many hospitals, but still she could not conceive. One day, however, *Min* Ogwal, who lived far away in Otwal village, had heard about Eripadica and come to see her.

At that time her son, Ogwal, was already seventeen.

Eripadica had cast her cowries on the *kworo* skin spread in front of her and read them. And her reading had been accurate. 'Do you know the large *opok* tree that stands behind the kitchen of the headmaster of Otwal Primary School?' Eripadica had asked *Min* Ogwal.

'No,' she had replied.

'When you go back home, visit the headmaster's home.'

'Yes, I will do that.'

'There is a big *opok* tree behind the headmaster's kitchen.'

'Yes.'

'There are two holes in the trunk of that *opok* tree. Are you listening?'

'Yes I am listening.'

'Now, when you find those holes, put your hand inside the upper hole and grope around. That is where your fertility is hidden.'

'Yes.'

'Can you remember who was present when your water broke before you gave birth to Ogwal?'

'Yes. There were two people, the midwife and my mother-in-law.'

'Where did you give birth?'

'In my own hut.'

'Well, then that means that the birth-water was not properly disposed of. Some wizard scooped up some of the soil in which it had sunk. Then she put it in a pot and hid it in the *opok* tree behind the kitchen of the headmaster of Otwal Primary School. That is where your fertility is hidden, in that big *opok* tree. Check inside the hole I told you about. And do not worry about snakes . Even if there is a snake inside the hole it will not bite you. It will not, I can assure you. And the pot will be there. When you find it, take it home and smash it on the ground. Then scatter both what it contains and the potsherds around. You will be able to conceive again. Are you listening?'

'I am listening,' *Min* Ogwal responded.

'If you are listening that is good. And now about paying me. If you do not conceive I will not want you to pay me anything. If you conceive, I will tell you what I want.' And she gave *Min* Ogwal some herbs 'to soften her womb and make it ready for a baby.'

On arriving back home, *Min* Ogwal had visited the *opok* tree, and sure enough there was a small pot inside it. She had taken the pot home and smashed it, scattering the contents and the potsherds in all directions.

Three months later *Min* Ogwal was pregnant.

Now Bitoroci and Alicinora knew that Eripadica was somebody you could trust.

The two women left their slippers at the entrance to Eripadica's work hut and entered. Eripadica bade them sit down. They sat down

125

opposite her, their legs stretched out in front of them. Between them and Eripadica was an old *kworo* skin.

'I am happy to see you,' Eripadica said.

'We thank you for welcoming us,' Bitoroci and Alicinora replied in unison.

'Will you tell me what brings you here, my agemates?' Eripadica enquired.

'Trouble,' Bitoroci said.

'Bad trouble,' Alicinora confirmed. 'Some people came in a car and took my son away. They had guns.'

'When was that?' Eripadica asked.

'Today,' Alicinora replied. 'This very night.'

'And now you want to know where he has been taken?' Eripadica asked.

'Yes,' Bitoroci replied, 'and also what has happened to him. Whether he is still alive, or whether he is dead.'

'Fine,' Eripadica said. Then she twisted round and grabbed up a fistful of cowries. She snatched up a gourd-rattle and shook it over the fist that held the cowries. Kwara-kwara...kwara-kwara...kwara-kwara...kwara-kwara... many times. Then she put her mouth to the cowrie hand and whispered to it. After that she jerked the cowrie hand up and down a number of times, then flung the cowries down onto the *kworo* skin.

The cowries rolled around, then stopped.

Some lay on their sides.

Others lay on their bellies.

Yet others lay on their backs.

Eripadica read the cowries while sucking her teeth. Noisily. Thk...thk...thk...thk...She gently finger-prodded the cowries, shifted them around, turned them over, all the time going thk...thk...thk...thk...

'Well,' she said, at last. 'My agemates, things are not very good.'

'Is Abudu dead?' Alicinora asked, alarmed.

Eripadica cast one more contemplative look at her cowries. 'No,' she said, 'Abudu is not dead. Not yet anyway. They may kill him. Or they may not. That is not so certain from these cowries. But what they show very clearly is that when he comes back, if he is coming back, he will have been kept away for a long time.'

126

'Has he been beaten?' Bitoroci asked, anxiety choking her.

Eripadica looked back at her cowries. Then she closed her eyes for some time. When she spoke her eyes were still closed.

'None of these cowries shows signs of Olwit pleading,' she said. 'I do not think Olwit has been beaten. Or hurt in any way.'

Chapter XIV

The hippo-hide whip went up and came down. Again and again and again. It lashed at Abudu Olwit, cutting into his back and arms and buttocks and head. And the grin on the face of his torturer became wider and wider, cutting a yellow-toothed gash in his face. Suddenly the grin became stiff and tormented, a mere baring of yellow teeth. Then the teeth became slimy and green and they began to fall out. His tormentor's body bloated up, first filling out his army brigadier's uniform. The fingers holding the whip grew fat and stiff with bloating. The whip stayed high up above Olwit, firmly held in the hand bloated and stiffened with putrefaction. Olwit grovelled on the ground, his arms raised and palms turned up in an attitude of prayer, pleading for mercy. Slowly the hand detached itself from the arm and came tumbling to the ground. Still gripping the whip, it landed with a soft, spongy thud. The brigadier's putrescent flesh slid off his face, very, very slowly, leaving bits of rotting flesh clinging to the bones, giving the skull a blotched, yellowish look. Then his knees buckled and he tumbled onto his back. He lay on the ground for a few moments before his bloated stomach started to rise. Then the stomach burst, and some of its contents splashed on Olwit's face.

Abudu Olwit screamed. Then he woke up.

Abudu Olwit was lying on his back on a cot in an army barracks. He had broken out in a cold sweat during the nightmare from which he had just woken.

Olwit had been detained in the barracks for three days now. Alone. In a small, stuffy room with only one stout-barred window high up in the western wall. The room was dark the whole day and only lightened up when the sun was about to set. Then the sun sent in yellowish-red shafts of light in which he sometimes saw little sparkling dots floating.

For company Olwit had only the green plastic toilet bucket and the coarse blanket on his bed.

Olwit was served two meals a day – a thin, sugarless maize gruel in the morning and lunch of beans and posho in the late afternoon. And nothing else. The food was passed to him through a hatch in the heavy metal door of his cell. Whenever the army private who served him his meals turned up at the hatch, Olwit asked him why he was being held there. Each time all the private did was cock his head, smile and then go away without so much as uttering a word.

The fourth day after Abudu Olwit's arrest, a sergeant unlocked his cell door and led him to the office of the garrison Intelligence Officer. The Intelligence Officer was a tall, lean man in his mid-thirties. He was a captain.

What the captain told Olwit made his jaw drop.

'W-w-what?!' Olwit stammered.

'You heard what I said,' the captain said. 'You have been accused of fomenting rebellion in Apac district.'

'Who told you that?'

'We have our sources. And we don't reveal them as a matter of principle.'

'My God!' Olwit exclaimed. 'So how am I supposed to be fomenting this rebellion?'

Abudu Olwit was surprised at how calm he was. He did not feel any fear. But he felt shock and the first hints of anger.

'You will learn the details soon,' the captain told him. 'And please do sit down.'

Olwit was not aware that he had been standing.

He sat down on the cushioned, straight-backed chair placed to the left of the captain's desk. The desk was grey and formica-topped.

The captain told him about how he had been using the resources of Alaro Prison Farm to facilitate the secret return of people who had worked in Bwete's army and intelligence service, so that they could destabilise the government. The captain said he knew two such people who had sneaked into the country, one from Zambia and the other from Canada. These two, he said, had scampered back into exile the moment they had heard about his arrest. Both men came from Teboke. Preliminary investigations had revealed that there was a groundswell of anger in Teboke against the government, the captain said, largely on account of the job losses many Teboke folk had suffered as a result of the disintegration of

129

Bwete's army and the privatisation of parastatals. That was what Abudu Olwit and his allies intended to tap into: the anger and resentment against the government. Olwit was widely respected and admired in Teboke and Alaro, the captain said, and he was therefore in a position to command the loyalties of a lot of people.

Abudu Olwit listened to all this with his mouth agape. And the longer he listened, the harder his stomach knotted. And the angrier he became. Since when did he begin taking an interest in active politics? Politics to him had been largely irrelevant, an area in which he took some intellectual interest and little else. Now why would he suddenly begin taking sides in politics even to the extent of instigating rebellion? As if he was not aware of the kind of background he came from? Coming from a past of such acute deprivation, pain and despair, he had had only one ambition in life: acquire a decent education, make some money, lead a life of relative comfort. Absolutely nothing else. He had never even remotely dreamt of fame, for he considered it largely a luxury. He had not thought of holding any kind of political office either. His ambitions did not lie in that direction at all! And now here he was being accused of serious political offences!

The captain intruded into Olwit's thoughts.

'Our investigations are still continuing,' the captain said, 'and we are working hand in hand with the police ... We have kept you here for three days. We don't want to keep you here any longer. We shall be moving you to a proper prison today.'

Abudu Olwit was immediately moved to the Lira central government prison. A month later he was transferred to Luzira Prisons in Kampala.

When his case came up in court for the first time two weeks later he was charged with sedition, plotting to overthrow a legitimately established government, embezzlement of government funds and use of government facilities for private profit. Olwit was to spend eighteen months on remand at Luzira Prisons before he was cleared of all charges brought against him for lack of conclusive evidence and witnesses. He was promptly acquitted.

It was as an inmate at Luzira Prisons that Olwit first heard about the Honourable Adoli-Awal's masterminding of his arrest and incarceration.

***

By the time Olwit was jailed, Saida Acola had been married to him for six years. She had not been particularly keen about marrying Olwit. Her mother, Bitoroci, had, however, argued with her, pleaded with her, wept before her until she had eventually succumbed to her wish.

'But I hardly know him,' Saida Acola had said.

'I closely watched him as he grew up,' Bitoroci lied. ' He is a good man. You will like him.'

'And will I learn to love him too?' Saida Acola asked.

Her mother barked out a short laugh. 'My daughter,' she said, 'look at me. I did not marry your father because I loved him. In our time we did not marry because of love. Nobody even talked about love then. I do not even understand the nature of this thing you call love. In our time, unless your people forced you to marry somebody, you chose a man because of his family, his character and his health. It was considered stupid for a girl to choose a man whose parents did not possess any animal wealth, for what would they use to pay your bridewealth? Bushrats? But you also looked at the family's health. Did they suffer from epilepsy, leprosy? Any disease that was likely to be inherited by your children?

'Even if a family had a lot of wealth, if it suffered from any serious disease it was shunned. Or if the family were known or suspected to be wizards, night dancers, poisoners or sorcerers. You also looked at a man's character – whether he was hardworking, kind, courageous, generous. And that was all. You never married because of this thing called love.'

'But times have changed, Mama,' Acola protested.

'Times have changed, I agree,' her mother replied irritably. 'Yes, times have changed, but human nature has not changed at all. Look around you. You will notice that the happiest homes are homes where there is enough food to eat, where nice clothes are easy to buy, where hardships are few. You are a woman like me, my daughter, and you should therefore know what a woman's heart yearns for.

131

You will not want a husband who rarely has enough money to buy nice clothes for you, to buy good things to eat, nice things for the children. You will not want a husband who cannot build a good house for you and your children to live in, for you to be proud of. You will not want a husband who cannot afford even a bicycle. Marriage is about wanting to dress, feed and live better than other women, to arouse their envy. Otherwise why do you think I chose your father? When he offered to marry me I was only nineteen, and he was already forty-eight and had four wives. I would have been stupid to turn him down, to turn down the life of comfort that his offer promised. Yes he is very old now, but I still am proud of him. Look what he has done for us. He has looked after us very well. He has sent you all to good schools. Look at the other people, people like Okullo Ipapalo and his wife. Scrounging for a living by selling pawpaws. Of course I could have married the man I liked most, Albino Ocen, who was only twenty-four at the time. Do you know Albino Ocen?'

'Yes I do.'

'And I know that you know the kind of work he does for a living. Making car-tyre sandals. Would you have been proud to have someone who makes car-tyre sandals as your father?'

Saida Achola looked down.

'My daughter,' Bitoroci said, 'I want you to understand one thing. I am not forcing you to marry Abudu Olwit, but think about it. Think about all the good things that can happen to you and to your children if you marry him. I barely knew your father when I married him, but I grew to like and respect him when I was already married to him. And he never beat me, not even once, though I was rather naughty as a young wife. Abudu Olwit is shy. You will not find it difficult to control him.'

Saida Acola sighed.

'Well, I am taking some millet to the grinding mill,' Bitoroci said, 'and at the mill I shall not pay for grinding my millet with love, but with money, money I have as a result of marrying your father. Think about it.'

Bitoroci rose slowly from the verandah of their sprawling house and walked away to the kitchen, leaving Saida Acola pondering. The more Acola thought, the more sharply she was struck by the validity of what her mother had said. She knew, or had heard of, a number of marriages that had foundered under the weight of poverty. The most remarkable was, however, that of Gaudensio Amute the primary school headmaster.

Gaudensio Amute had married Maria Acio when things were still very good for teachers. He was one of the very few people in Teboke at that time who owned a Volkswagen Beetle, locally called 'Tortoise', a tape recorder and a stereo record player. He was very young then, barely twenty-eight, and already a headmaster. He had given Maria Acio's parents ten cows and six goats, in addition to other things, as bridewealth. After the customary marriage process was concluded, he had proceeded to wed Maria Acio in church, something very rare in Lango then. And he and his Maria had been happy living together in the school where they both taught. They were a model couple, and were often to be seen strolling hand-in-hand towards Okole swamp, or plucking wild flowers and giving them to each other to smell. The local people called them 'Europeans'.

Then Idi had wrested state power from Bwete and a few years later the Ugandan economy had collapsed.

Soon afterwards headmaster Gaudensio Amute's Volkswagen 'Tortoise' got parked in his garage because he could afford neither new tyres nor fuel. Then the record player fell silent because he could not afford dry cells. And the tape recorder at first played only the same, hackneyed songs until it, too, fell silent for lack of dry cells and spares.

The locals did not see Gaudensio Amute and his wife strolling hand-in-hand towards Okole swamp any more. Instead, Amute had taken to drinking *arege* by the bottleful – every day.

And people began hearing that fights took place between Gaudensio Amute and Maria at least once every week, violent, closed-door fights in which plates and furniture got broken and their three children sometimes got hit. Then one afternoon in November, with the sun sending down vicious shafts of torrid heat, Maria had shot screaming out of her house like a nightjar and fled towards the staffroom, with her panga-wielding husband in hot pursuit. It took

133

the strenuous and unremitting effort of all the male staff to restrain Gaudensio from hacking Maria to death.

When Idi was ejected from State House by Tanzanian troops and Ugandan guerrillas, things had become so bad between Gaudensio Amute and Maria Acio that they rarely talked to each other, and she no longer cooked for him. A few months after Idi's fall, Maria left Gaudensio Amute for a Tanzanian private soldier, a Muslim from Musoma. Gaudensio's and Maria's much-lauded marriage had died, and now it lay splattered on the hard, jagged rock of adversity like a hapless mosquito.

Saida Acola's mother had told her this story herself as a warning about the dangers that poverty posed to marriage.

But was money, was wealth the most important thing in a marriage? Acola wondered. Why were there so many wealthy homes with so much unhappiness, where the women often desperately flung themselves at other men? What were they seeking then if they had everything that they wanted? Had they become so greedy that what would have been sufficient for everybody else was not quite sufficient for them? Or were they seeking the kind of affection and appreciation they could not get from their husbands, affection and appreciation that they ardently craved? What exactly were they looking for? Happiness? Did happiness really exist? If it did, in what form did it exist? Could one point at it and say: This is happiness, this is the form it takes? If happiness really did exist, in what hard kernel did it lie nestled so that one could crack the kernel open, pluck it out, press it to one's breast and say: I have found happiness, now I am happy? What made a marriage happy? What made LIFE itself happy?

***

Saida Acola's first meeting with Abudu Olwit had been a particularly nervous affair. The meeting had been arranged by her own mother, Bitoroci, and Olwit's mother, Alicinora. She had met many men before, but none quite as diffident as Olwit.

Saida Acola had expected Olwit to perform much better since he was already in his early thirties. And since he was an Assistant Superintendent of Prisons in charge of a whole prison farm, Namalu

Prison Farm, and thus had a large number of men at his beck and call.

The meeting had occurred when she was in a three-week vacation from Uganda College of Commerce Pakwach and Olwit was on a visit to his mother. It had taken place in Olwit's mother's home where he had constructed an oblong grass-thatched house for himself. It had taken place inside the house, late on a Thursday afternoon.

They had exchanged greetings, and then Olwit had fallen silent. As the birds twittered and rustled among the branches of the trees behind the oblong grass-thatched house Olwit spoke. 'I hear you are a student of Uganda College of Commerce Pakwach,' he said, looking over the top of her head at the roof of the house.

'Yes,' she said, demurely.

'What are you studying?' he asked. He still looked distracted.

'Marketing,' she responded.

'Mm,' he said and fell silent again. He brought his eyes down from the roof and settled them on her, quizzical and contemplative. His chin rested on his left wrist. She looked into his eyes for a few moments, then looked down at the floor smeared with cow dung.

'How do you find your job?' she ventured, starting to crack her finger joints.

'Boring,' he answered. 'I never really wanted to work in the Prisons Service. But you know what things are like these days.'

His eyes were now focused on her. They looked dreamy, yet intense. He seemed to be thinking a lot of thoughts.

It was now her turn to look up at the rafters of the thatch roof. She went on cracking her finger joints. Abudu Olwit did not even make an attempt to get near to her. He sat detached on his low cane stool as she sat on hers. Occasionally he squinted at her, narrowing his eyes and gazing at her from behind the safety of his fat eyelids. She stayed put, partly because she pitied him and did not wish to hurt his feelings, and partly because she did not want to let down her mother. So they went on with their jerky, insipid conversation...

But that was about six years ago. Now she was his wife and had borne him two children. Though their marriage had been a dull, boring, passionless affair at the beginning, an appreciable amount of affection

135

and mutual admiration had grown between them. Saida Acola considered herself reasonably happy in her marriage...

And now Abudu Olwit was in jail. She felt a deep and paralysing loneliness, a loneliness that often made her sit on the verandah of their sprawling house at Alaro Prison Farm and stare emptily into space for hours. It was a loneliness that stabbed and wrenched at her heart, that made it shrink and cramp, that made her choke and pant. And sometimes in the morning she would fail to summon the energy, and will, to rise up from her bed. So she would go on lying in her bed, her heart still and arid with longing and her face drenched in tears.

The first time she visited Olwit in jail was the second day after his transfer from the military jail to the Lira central government prison. She was allowed to speak to him through a small window fitted with stout steel bars.

She took both her children, Oula, a boy, and Awino, a girl, with her. Oula was five and Awino, three.

When he was summoned and appeared on the other side of the window, she felt the tears welling up behind her eyes. She told herself: Do not cry. Look, you are going to cry in front of these men who, if they had been at Alaro Prison Farm, would have been under your husband's charge. And all the while she was looking down towards the floor, at the top of Oula's head, and struggling to hold back the tears .

'Saida,' she heard his voice call out her name, close and distant at the same time. She looked up and noticed his hand holding that of their daughter, whom she was cradling in her right arm. The child was chattering away happily, obviously very happy and excited to see her father for the first time in almost a week. Awino had taken hold of her father's arm with her small, dimply hand.

Saida looked at the haunted look on his haggard face and whatever little self-control she had mustered simply crumbled.

And she wept.

And at first Abudu Olwit just stood there, on his side of the window, gazing at her. And then his own eyes glazed over, and they got wet, and the tears flowed, coming in large, warm drops.

If Olwit had been an ordinary prisoner, he would have been dragged back into the inaccessible belly of the prison and Saida Acola ordered to go back home and come back another day. But he was no ordinary prisoner, being an Assistant Superintendent of Prisons. So they were allowed to weep for as long as they wanted. After they were finished with weeping they wiped their eyes dry, Olwit with the back of his right hand and Saida with her green *kitenge* wrapper.

'I am happy you have come to see me,' he said, snivelling.

She did not respond. She opened her mouth but no sound came forth. So she just gazed at him, her large, tear-reddened eyes beginning to fill up again.

'Please do not start weeping again,' Olwit begged.

Saida Acola dabbed at her eyes with one corner of her wrapper and placed Awino down on the floor. Then she lifted Oula up so that he could greet his father, whom he so much resembled.

The moment he took his father's hand into his he piped up, 'Daddy, who brought you here?'

'Do not ask your daddy such questions, Oula,' Saida rebuked.

Oula looked at her, a quizzical expression on his face.

'Do not stop him,' Olwit said to Saida, a thin, tired smile coming on his face. 'He is too young to understand.'

'How long will you be here?' she asked.

The prison warder standing behind Olwit cleared his throat.

Olwit turned and looked at him, a questioning expression on his face.

The warder understood his question before he could ask it. 'Yes, time is up,' the warder said. 'But I can give you a little more time.'

'How much more?' Olwit asked.

'About two minutes.'

'Only?'

'Only.'

'Fine,' Olwit said. 'Saida, when you go back, greet my mother and my mother-in-law. Tell them that life in jail is not easy, but that I will get out, for I have done nothing wrong. And look after these children well.'

'I will,' she promised. 'I have brought you some food. And also

137

some money. I have given them to Corporal Opolot.'

'Thank you.'

'Time up!' the warder said.

Olwit glanced at the warder, then turned back to Saida Acola. 'Please go back home now,' he said. 'I will not die.'

'Stay well,' she said. 'I miss you.' And her eyes misted over.

Olwit released Oula's hand and retracted his arm. Saida Acola picked up Awino and flung her on her back, fastening her firmly with the *kitenge* wrapper. When she was through, she straightened up. Olwit was gone.

Saida Acola took hold of Oula's hand and shuffled out of the visitors' room towards the large double steel doors of the prison entrance. The warder at the door opened it for her and she stepped out into the bright afternoon sun. She crossed the road that separated the prison from the police lines and stood under a leafy mango tree to wait for transport to town. Little birds twittered and flitted among the leaves of the tree.

A few minutes later Saida Acola waved down a *boda-boda* motorcycle. The motorcycle taxi took her to town, from where she caught a pick-up taxi back home.

That day, after she had put the children to bed, Saida Acola went out and sat on the northern verandah of her house at Alaro Prison Farm. She gazed up at the black night sky and marvelled at the yellow sickle-blade of moon hanging lone and mournful near the rim of the inverted bowl of star-decked sky. In the distance a number of tree branches pressed their deeper blackness, sometimes leafy, sometimes gaunt and skeletal, into the vast star-washed expanse of black sky.

Saida Acola felt even lonelier.

Chapter XV

Teboke.

The ginnery had collapsed a few years earlier, and Major General Idi was still the national president. Time had rapidly flowed, invigorating, fructifying, blunting, wreaking havoc–but mostly wreaking havoc.

Fr Guglielmo Varasco had stayed in Teboke for six years. During that period he had established an orchard, a poultry unit, a crop farm, a grinding mill and an old people's home. And in the process also established a firm and unshakeable reputation for a completely unpredictable temper and an ardent love for litigation. Then he had departed as suddenly as he had come, taking a young Lango woman with him. Some time after Fr Varasco's departure, a rumour began to spread that, on arrival back in Italy, he had quit the priesthood and taken his Lango woman to the altar.

Fr Varasco was succeeded by an aging priest, sixty-five-year-old Marcellino Luigi. Fr Luigi's first assignment in Teboke seemed to have been to get rid of all the inmates of the old people's home and to ensure that the farm reverted to bush. The first casualty of his indifference to farming was the mission tractor, which soon stopped running owing to lack of spares. Fr Luigi was also famous for his voracious appetite. This earned him the nickname 'Tua'. A *tua* is a handwoven, mud-plastered food storage bin, often the size of a small fridge. Fr Luigi's stomach seemed to have the capacity to take in as much food as a *tua* on any given day. Shortly after his arrival, all that was left of the poultry unit was the oblong *mabati* structure that once housed the birds. Fr Luigi had worked his way through the birds like a civet cat.

A few months after Fr Luigi's arrival many mission workers left, for they could not stand his overweening self-centredness and his cold aloofness. Among the first to leave was Dempterio Arim, the young catechist who had trained himself to speak his mother tongue, Lango, with a strong Italian accent. Soon after giving up his catechist's job, Arim's accent straightened itself out. Arim also rapidly graduated into the premier league of Teboke's heavy *arege* drinkers, which made his very red gums seem even redder.

139

Teboke Elementary School, which had been the shining pride of Cegere sub-county, looked dejected and forlorn, its impoverished teachers the butt of jokes by Teboke farmer and trader folk, the sap of respectability having been drained off the teaching profession by worsening poverty and penury. Most of the school's good teachers, hurt, bewildered and demoralised, had either quit teaching to do *magendo* – black marketeering – or gone off to other countries to seek better fortunes there. The maths wizard Oluma-Odoo, for example, had fled to Nigeria. After Idi's fall, Oluma-Odoo would return to Uganda armed with a master's degree in Computer Programming and another master's in Education and thereafter land an impressive job at Crested Towers, Uganda's Ministry of Education headquarters. Alfred Opio, the music teacher, had been driven by ridicule to first take up farming and later seek solace in the bottle. As he slouched around his home village, Acaba, looking disconsolate and disoriented, people taunted him about his habit of always carrying his flute with him. They called him *Olwet*, Flute. He later sought refuge in Kenya, but his wife refused to join him there. Finding Kenya a lonely and inconvenient country, he proceeded to Tanzania. Here he joined Kikoosi Maalum, one of the armed exile groups that would fight to dislodge Idi. After Lango had fallen to the combined force of Tanzanian troops and Ugandan exiles, Alfred Opio, now a full lieutenant, drove to Acaba in a commandeered Fiat Campagnola, to check on his people. He discovered that his wife, Kerobina, had already been inherited by one of his younger brothers, and that she was pregnant with his third child. His own children, Odongo and Acen, were already in their late teens. When they were told he was their father they looked at him very strangely, and seemed not to be particularly enthusiastic about seeing him. Alfred Opio's mother had died of malaria three years before, and his father had gone blind. When Opio introduced himself to his father, the old man said: 'Thank you for coming back. Do you have some money for me to buy some tobacco and a drink?' Opio pressed a few banknotes into his father's hand and bade him goodbye. Then he got back into the Fiat and drove off. A year and a half later a landmine blew off his lower jaw and left arm in Luweero, where a war was raging between

140

government troops and anti-government guerillas. He was buried at the soldiers' cemetery in Jinja.

Life had become increasingly difficult in Teboke. Basic commodities such as salt, sugar and soap were difficult to come by and the people had to use their ingenuity to produce substitutes. Goat droppings were burnt and strained through water to 'manufacture' salt. Cut-up pieces of sugar cane were pounded in wooden mortars and the resulting liquid transferred directly into hot water, frequently without tea or coffee. But they still called it *chai*, tea. People dug up the roots of the *ilila* plant and used it as soap. Soon whole villages had run out of *ilila* and people had to make do with pawpaw leaves, which often left the hands of the user raw and chapped. Signposts were pulled up and beaten into hoes.

There is one incident that the people of Teboke will never forget. It happened during the fifth year of Idi's rule. Around the middle of that year, the Provincial Administrator of the Northern Province, a young Uganda Army brigadier, turned up unannounced in a convoy of one green army Benz (the brigadier's), a green canvas-covered Landrover (the brigadier's bodyguards') and a large covered truck whose cargo no-one had any clue about. It turned out the cargo was hoes, and the brigadier had accompanied them in order to supervise their sale. People were ordered to line up and buy only one hoe each. The brigadier stood next to the hoe salesman in his new, well-pressed brigadier's uniform as the line slowly inched forward. He gently rapped his canvas puttees and brilliant black shoes with a short hippo-hide whip held in his right hand. A holstered pistol was strapped to his belt. His bodyguards lounged around behind him, they too armed with guns and hippo-hide whips.

When the hoes allocated for Teboke seemed to be getting depleted, however, the line dissolved into a stampede. The brigadier ordered his men to bring the stampede under control. He led the assault on the people, viciously laying into them with his whip as his minions followed suit. The people fled the hoe-sales area and stood gathered across the street like frightened goats, watchful and bunched together. The brigadier shouted across the road. He told the people that since they had failed to behave themselves, they did not deserve to buy any more hoes. Then he ordered his bodyguards to load the remaining hoes back into the box-body truck. The moment the loading was done, the brigadier got back into his dark-green Benz and the convoy crawled off towards Cegere.

During these difficult times, it became impossible to celebrate Independence Day and Christmas properly. Before, either one slaughtered a cow for one's family or a small number of people came together and bought a cow. They would usually not be more than six or seven. They would carry big sackfuls of meat back to their homes. But now people had to be content with a kilo or two of beef. Or they ate chicken.

Widows and orphans increased in number. The first explosion in widow and orphan numbers occurred when, two years into Major General Idi's rule, some eighty young men – and not so young ones– were boozed up and lured onto trucks. They were told that they would be ferried to Tanzania via Sudan so they could fight and topple Idi from outside. A few miles inside Sudan they found some strange armed men waiting for them. Their hosts gave them hoes and spades and ordered them to dig a large, shallow pit. Then the hosts blindfolded them and hacked and bludgeoned them to death, the pit that they had dug becoming their grave. Only two of them survived, both badly cut. One died of blood poisoning on his way back to Uganda. The other arrived home with ridge-like scars all over his body and told whoever would listen that all the people he had travelled to Sudan with had been hacked and bludgeoned to death. No-one was ready to believe him, so they instead reported him to Idi's intelligence service. He had to flee Teboke and go into hiding in Gulu town, where a large truck ran him over barely three months later. With no-one to claim his mangled body from the Gulu Hospital mortuary, he had to be buried at the Gulu Town Council cemetery.

Even when Bwete returned to power things did not become good. There was bitterness in people's hearts and bewilderment in their heads. What had happened to their husbands? the widows asked. What had happened to their fathers? the orphans wondered. And widows' committees were set up and some good people living across the waters sent over money and material things to help them. Suddenly there were 'widows' all over the place, and the more enlightened 'widows' appropriated for themselves what was meant for the real widows.

But still things did not become good.

Still there were few things in the shops, and still they were not cheap.

Still the teachers earned barely enough to buy a decent pair of trousers or dress, and still there were no drugs in the dispensary.

Still people walked around in rags, and still they farmed cotton and sunflower and potatoes and cassava and millet and beans and pigeon peas using the hand-hoe. And now the cotton that they sold to the cooperative societies did not benefit them at all, for there now was a long line of starved and sharp-toothed cheats running from the cotton buying centres right up to the district headquarters of the cooperative movement, each one of them wanting something to eat. And now there was no threat of a Langi-hating Idi. Instead, there was some money flowing down from the line Ministry in Kampala directly to the cooperative officials in Lango who took the peasants' cotton for free and told the peasants there was no money. And the hapless peasants waited for their money, angry and bitter and broke, and not knowing who to turn to for redress. And the self-same officials said: 'Look, are you not happy now that you are free? With Idi gone, why should you be complaining?' Then they sharpened their teeth some more and waited for next year's cotton harvest and the next. And they got fatter, and did not pay the cotton farmers a cent. Till the farmers got tired of growing cotton in order to fatten other people and took up the growing of other crops instead. Crops such as sunflower and simsim which they could sell to the traders or oil processors direct. And the cooperative officials grumbled: 'Look, we were trying to help the government to repair the shattered economy through the exportation of cotton, a very important cash crop indeed. Now look what these peasants have gone and done. Put acre upon acre of land under crops that do not benefit the nation much. They are unpatriotic!' And the stomachs of the cooperative officials began to shrink and recede, for there was now no longer as much to eat as there had been but a short while earlier. And the officials attempted to exhort people to return to growing cotton.

143

GROW COTTON! they urged over public address systems. GROW COTTON! they shouted through adverts pasted on walls and trees and electric poles and telephone poles. GROW MORE COTTON! they wrote on the backs and sides of Leyland and Tata and Bedford trucks. But the peasant farmers stayed 'unpatriotric', and they refused to go back to growing cotton. And the peasants drank more and fewer of their children went to school.

Then General Ragamoi's soldiers struck and president Bwete had to go into exile again. Teboke became poorer, quieter, more bewildered. And people slept around more, and drank even more, and went to school less. And they complained in the assumed safety of their houses – grass-thatched or *mabati*-roofed – and whispered with fear whenever an army vehicle passed, or whenever an arrogant soldier rode by on a bicycle or motorcycle.

Then Uchebi came out of Luweero and took over from General Ragamoi. And the people were even more frightened, wondering what would happen to them since he was an *anam*. And they slept around much more and went to school much less. Bewilderment and desolation hung over Teboke like a dark cloud roiling with poison. Soon people began to hear about the fighting and deaths at Corner Kilak in Gulu district. Before long there was fighting in Teboke too, fighting between rebels – those from far away and home-grown ones – and government troops. And there were deaths and there was destruction. The world appeared to be a very unpromising place indeed, so the people slept with whoever they could lay their hands on. They also boozed on *arege* and *wiri* and *acoi* beer. And they forgot school even more.

When the war was over they collected the scattered pieces of their broken lives together and tried to work out where to start from.

They hoed their gardens. And they planted and weeded and thinned and harvested, and they ate or sold the crops.

They repaired their shattered homes as best they could.

They resumed sending their children to school to sit on mud floors and write in the dirt. And to snigger at and insult the penniless, ill-clad teachers...

Then the people began to go down with the disease that they had mostly only heard about. It was not the disease that made the glands

144

in your groin explode – *gurunet*. No, it was not *gurunet*. It did not make one's manhood or womanhood weep with pus either, or a woman's waist burn and ache. No. They had first heard about this disease as a disease of a far-away place called Rakai, a disease that was caused by bewitchment. They had heard that the disease had travelled to Kampala and Entebbe and Jinja, and that it had set down deep roots there. But from Teboke to Rakai, or Kampala, or Entebbe, or Jinja was such a long, long distance. So this disease was not likely to reach Teboke. But then soon people began to pass bits of their intestines in their stools. And to develop warts on their mouths, and large, deep wounds in their legs and soles. When some of them got so thin that the veins in their bodies stood out like beer-sucking tubes and their eardrums ruptured, the people of Teboke knew that the disease had arrived. They knew that the disease that when you were fat first made you trim, then thin, and then ate you up had arrived – and that it had come to stay. They knew that it was *two jonyo*, 'the *thin* disease'.

Abudu Olwit had lived through some of these bad times, and had watched some of his former schoolmates go down with the *thin* disease. He had washed his clothes with the roots of the *ilila* plant instead of soap. He had eaten saltless food. He had received treatment from traditional healers and medicine men instead of those trained in the skills and ways of the white man's medicine. His skin had been incised and herbs rubbed into it ... Stones, bits of bone and dry grass, hair and teeth had been sucked out of his flesh ... He had imbibed cupfuls of foul-tasting liquid concoctions ... All this in the name of trying to get well; and because there were no drugs in the local dispensary. He had never had really nice clothes to wear at school and university. His first pair of leather shoes had come when he was already in Senior Three. He had been insulted and taunted and teased and put down by his own mother and other people. He had played hide-and-seek with both government soldiers and rebels. His graduation from university had pushed all these pains and memories into those regions of his mind where he could not focus too much on them. He had felt happy, excited. And he had been grateful, though not exactly content, for being an Assistant

145

Superintendent of Prisons, and for being in charge of Namalu Prison Farm, and later Alaro Prison Farm.

None of Abudu Olwit's many sufferings and deprivations had, however, prepared him at all for the sufferings and deprivations of prison.

He loathed the prison food. The bad food that at the beginning made one's stomach run for days on end. The unchanging menu of poorly cooked beans and posho. Though, because of his job, the prison warders considered him as one of their own, and sympathised with him on account of the circumstances that had led to his arrest and incarceration, there was little they could do to help make his life easier. He had to share the food and money that his wife occasionally brought with his fellow prisoners. He was often bullied into sharing them by hardened jailbirds who gave him nothing in return.

He loathed the coarse sisal mat and rough prison blanket that were steamed in large metal drums once every month to rid them of voracious lice and bedbugs.

He loathed the overcrowding in the prison wards, its stuffy and stifling air.

But above all he loathed the restrictions, the highly controlled lifestyle. You could not do whatever you wanted to do at whatever time. It was this lack of freedom, this feeling of helplessness, this feeling that while you had been put away, shut away behind the walls of a prison, others were going about their normal lives – working, making money, advancing their careers, having normal sex – it was this that really hurt.

Chapter XVI

Abudu Olwit arrived back home from jail on a Tuesday morning. He was accompanied by his wife and two children.

When Saida Acola had been informed about her husband's impending release from jail, she had hurried off to Kampala and pitched camp there to await his release. Olwit's release had come a full ten days after her arrival. The sight of Olwit's drawn and haggard face had made her drop to her knees and weep tears of hurt and happiness. Hurt because of the pain she knew he had suffered in jail; happiness because he was back with her at last. After such a long absence, he had come back to her at last – to her and *their* children. From Luzira Prisons a friend had offered Olwit and his family a lift to Buganda Bus Park in the centre of Kampala. From the bus park they had caught a bus to Corner Loro, situated five miles away from Teboke. When Olwit and his family arrived at his mother's home, he was surprised by the number of people who had assembled to welcome him back and to commiserate with him about his imprisonment. It was early afternoon.

Abudu Olwit found his mother, Alicinora, seated on the projecting end of one of the floor-logs of her hand-woven granary, her chin cradled in her palms. For once she was sober. Even as the other women ululated and hopped around in a dance of welcome, eddying around him like crested cranes, Alicinora did not rise. It was only after Saida Acola had brought a folding chair from Alicinora's sleeping hut and bidden Olwit sit down that Alicinora got up and approached Olwit. Straight as a pole and dignified, the heat-cracked soles of her broad feet rising and falling with precision. When she arrived where her son was seated, Alicinora knelt before him and shook his hands with both hers. Then she opened out his right hand and spat onto the palm.

'I thank God for bringing you back,' she said, her voice whispery.

'Life was very difficult in jail, mother,' Olwit said.

'I know,' Alicinora responded.

'There they treat you like a dog. Like you do not have a mother,' Olwit added.

'You are thin, my son,' Alicinora said. 'They must have treated you worse than something without a mother.'

'And I worried a lot, mother. I worried about you and about Saida and our two children. I worried a lot.'

'I can see it in your face, son.'

'And I was imprisoned for nothing.'

'Not for nothing, son. Adoli-Awal was jealous. He had become jealous of the good things you were doing for the people.'

'But I did not mean him any harm, mother.'

'That is what the world is like, son. Sometimes it is actually better to intend harm, for if you were to suffer for it, you would have little to regret.'

The only occurrence that had shocked the Honourable Adoli-Awal as much as the release of Abudu Olwit from jail was possibly the first overthrow of Bwete from the Ugandan presidency about twenty years earlier. Adoli-Awal had thought that, in view of the gravity of the charges brought against him, Olwit would stay in prison for much longer than he did. He was sure that Abudu Olwit knew who was responsible for his arrest and imprisonment. He was aware that Abudu Olwit had become something of a hero owing to the support he had given to the people in his constituency when they were famine-stricken, and that this popularity represented substantial political capital. The only thing he was not sure of was whether Olwit had the desire – and the will– to make a bid for his parliamentary seat.

Before Olwit's arrest Adoli-Awal had warned him about what might befall him if he did not stop 'this foolishness of thinking that you can unseat me'.

It was on one of his rare visits home that Adoli-Awal had mounted his attack. And Adoli-Awal had not been patient enough to first take him aside and talk to him as one adult to another. Adoli-Awal had followed him to Namu's bar-restaurant at 6.00 p.m. on a Sunday and delivered his attack right there and then, in the presence of his fellow drinkers and at the top of his deep voice. Even despite the jeering and booing of some of the drinkers, Adoli-Awal would not shut up. And he had delivered his attack standing up.

'My son,' Adoli-Awal had said, 'as far as politics is concerned, you are no more than a little child with snot in his nose. You may be thinking that since you are a grown-up now and since you run a whole prison farm you are now a man. My son, I want to tell you today, as far as politics is concerned, you are not yet one.'

These words had deeply baffled Abudu Olwit. For a few moments he could not work out the import of what Adoli-Awal was talking about. He had never told anybody that he wanted to run for parliament. He had never even thought of running for parliament. And now here he was being publicly accused of wanting to usurp somebody's parliamentary seat.

'I am not really interested in standing for parliament, Adoli-Awal,' Olwit replied.

'You are,' Adoli-Awal replied, pointedly. 'You may not say it with your mouth, but what you have been doing in Teboke and Alemi shows clearly that you are.' And Adoli-Awal went on to talk about the water-pumps that had been installed in his constituency through Olwit's influence. If Olwit meant no harm, why did he not inform him about what he intended to do, even seek his co-operation? Why did he sneak behind his back and have boreholes sunk without his knowledge, and yet he knew full well that he was the one representing the people who would drink the water from the boreholes in the national parliament? Now he had also heard that Olwit was using the resources of Alaro Prison Farm to try to impress the Teboke and Alemi people even more. Olwit had become the one person who never missed a burial in these places. Even the burials of very little children. As if he was the only person that God had endowed with the capacity to grieve. Well, let Olwit go ahead with his plans. He, Mike Adoli-Awal, son of *Rwot* Awal whose eyes never blinked in fear, would see who would win in the end.

Then Adoli-Awal had got back into his Toyota Landcruiser and sped away.

Abudu Olwit had been quite shocked by Adoli-Awal's verbal attack on him.

Abudu Olwit had wondered what designs Adoli-Awal harboured. He knew that he, Olwit, had never had much interest in active politics.

149

His interest in that area of national life was limited to purely academic discussions of the merits and demerits of the various leaders Uganda had had since independence, and of the strengths and weaknesses of government policies and programmes. And that was all. All his life Abudu Olwit had tried to hew what little happiness he could from the hard rock of adversity and human existence. Now that he had scored some measure of success, he expected to be permitted to enjoy it.

It was only after his arrest and during his incarceration that Abudu Olwit would realise that Adoli-Awal's threat had been in earnest.

**

The sordidness of prison life led Olwit to one of the most important resolutions of his life. He decided that he would go into active politics the moment he was released from jail. He swore that he would make absolutely sure that Adoli-Awal felt the weight of his political presence. He also swore to give a big shake to the parliamentary seat to which Adoli-Awal seemed to have become so deeply accustomed, which he seemed to believe was his by birthright, and see if the bastard did not spill off the seat and land on his lean backside.

Olwit was angry and vengeful, and felt deep down that he could turn his nascent popularity in Teboke and Alemi into formidable political capital. He would then find out if, as Adoli-Awal believed about himself, he was too stout a tree to be felled by a mere hoe.

150

Chapter XVII

That year's campaigns for the national parliament would be hot. And everybody knew this. They knew that Olwit was bringing a lot of prison anger to the campaigns, and that Adoli-Awal would deploy all the skills he had acquired over the years in an attempt to retain his seat.

It was the campaigns for the third national parliament since president Uchebi came to power fifteen years earlier. There was only one person competing for Adoli-Awal's constituency besides Abudu Olwit and Adoli-Awal himself. This third candidate was called Luka Apel, a senior employee in the Ministry of Commerce. A lot of the people in the constituency knew Luka Apel's name, but few knew much else about him, or had laid eyes on him. When Major General Idi had been chased from Ugandan soil about twenty years earlier, Luka Apel had been one of the Ugandan refugees who had returned to Uganda from neighbouring Tanzania, where he had graduated with a Bachelor of Statistics degree from the University of Dar es Salaam barely two years earlier. His degree, as well as his firm and vocal support for ex-president Bwete, had earned him the big job in the Ministry of Commerce after Bwete regained the national presidency. Both Luka Apel and Bwete had been forced to take up exile in Tanzania by the depredations of the hulking Major General Idi, who had unseated Bwete in one of the most brutal coups in Africa. Between the time he acquired that job and the start of the campaigns for the Uchebi administration's third parliament, however, Luka Apel had been to his home village, Cegere, only five times. All the five times he had put up at luxurious hotels in Lira town, instead of with his parents.

Luka Apel's contempt for country folk was well known. Furthermore, he did not have a house in the village. It was rumoured that he had built two houses in Kampala, one for his Tanzanian wife and the other for his Ugandan wife, and that he was planning to build a third one in Lira town. But none in his home village. A man who did not even think of building a house in his home village could not be considered one of them, even if he was born and raised among them, the villagers concluded. The villagers had heard that Apel had a lot of money, so they wondered why he could not build a house in his own village, and why he could not come home more frequently, even if only to attend burials. They were not going to vote for him, they decided. How could they vote for someone who, as far as they were concerned, had turned himself into a foreigner?

The Honourable Adoli-Awal knew that as far as politics in his constituency was concerned, Luka Apel was a complete nonentity. So he was not at all bothered about him. To him Luka Apel was like a man who turned up at an *ikoce* dance decked out in suit and tie, and well-shined leather shoes, instead of the mandatory shorts, vest and car-tyre sandals or gumboots. With what amount of vigour would he do the *ikoce* dance in his heat-absorbing suit? And which girl would want to dance with him, since they would suspect him of hiding some strange disease in his suit? Adoli-Awal considered his constituents to be like the girls at an *ikoce* dance, who would not pick you on the basis of how expensively dressed you were, but rather because you were both appropriately dressed, and were an impressive dancer. As far as he could see, Luka Apel had failed on both counts. Abudu Olwit, on the other hand, was both appropriately dressed and seemed prepared to dance as well as he, Adoli-Awal.

He therefore decided that during his campaign he would try his best not to refer to Luka Apel at all, but if he had to refer to him at all, then he would say 'that man'.

Abudu Olwit; however, he would deal with differently. Dealing with him would be like spear-hunting catfish at night. If you wanted to kill as many catfish as possible, the first one that you attacked was not the lead catfish but the one that brought up the rear. If you attacked the catfish at the head of the procession, the rest would whip around and flee. It was likely that you would return home with only that catfish. If you were lucky that is. You could even miss it and go back home empty-handed. But if you started with the catfish at the rear of the procession, you could work your way deftly forward. By the time the lead catfish realised that there was something wrong, it might be the only one left, probably with a fish-spear poised over its trunk.

152

He would deal with Abudu Olwit the way one skinned a monitor lizard, Adoli-Awal thought. If you wanted to end up with a neat, undamaged skin you started the skinning at the tail and progressed carefully towards the head. When you reached the head, all you had to do was peel the skin off the head.

Abudu Olwit had to be speared like a catfish, with cunning and stealth; he had to be skinned like a monitor lizard, with a great deal of deftness.

It was a directive from the national government that all the candidates in a constituency hold joint campaign meetings. The first two meetings that the candidates held at Olo-lango and Agong villages passed without trouble. At both the meetings those in attendance asked a number of difficult questions. For instance, they asked Adoli-Awal about what important things he thought he had done for them since he was first elected to parliament. Abudu Olwit, on the other hand, they asked what he intended to do for them that he thought Adoli-Awal could not do. Luka Apel they mostly asked about where he was hailing from, where he had hidden himself all these years, and why he had decided to stand in 'their' constituency, yet they did not 'properly' know him.

The first hint of trouble appeared during the third meeting, which took place at Teboke trading centre. The venue was the group of old mango trees in front of two big *mabati* houses. The Indians who had set up and run the now-defunct cotton ginnery had lived in these houses.

It was early afternoon. The sun sent down blistering waves of heat that weaved and shimmered and hurt people's eyes. The heat made the murram road traversing the trading centre hot enough to bake an egg on.

A large number of people gathered to listen to the candidates. Many of them had broken off bunches of leaves and were waving them over their heads in a futile attempt to ward off the heat. Some of them were too drunk to be able to remember their own names.

Teboke folks had brought out the best seats they could find for the parliamentary candidates and their campaign managers. Sofas that had not been used for a long time for fear that children might

153

damage them were dusted and brought out for the first time. Also new ones. The parliamentary candidates and their campaign managers sat in the sofas, with Abudu Olwit and Mike Adoli-Awal eyeing each other with ill-disguised hostility and suspicion. Their campaign managers did not talk to each other. The two candidates largely ignored the third candidate, Luka Apel.

Adoli-Awal was the first to be asked to speak. He got up slowly, taking full advantage of his impressive height. Then he wiped his glasses with an impeccable white handkerchief, put them back over his eyes, cleared his throat. Then he spoke.

'My people,' he said, 'I feel bad talking to you today under these trees as if I do not have a large compound of my own where you could have gathered to listen to me.' He glanced at Abudu Olwit. 'If it had not been because of government ordering that we all address you together, I would have invited you all to my home, along with Abudu Olwit and that other man – I keep forgetting his name –'

'Apul,' a woman in the crowd offered.

'Apel,' a man's voice corrected her.

'Apul or Apel,' Adoli-Awal said. 'Well, I do not think it is very important anyway. As I was saying, I would have invited you all, including Abudu Olwit and Apul, and talked to you in my own home, not under some old mango trees.

'I do not want to talk much about myself. I am a mature man, my father was born here, my grandfather was also born here. And most of you know where they are both buried.' He pointed in the direction of the place where both the men lay buried. 'In Abari,' he said. 'That is where they lie buried. And they were both men of achievement.' He cleared his throat. 'I do not like boasting, but I must tell you that I come from a sound, respected family. When I look around me, however, I sometimes wonder whether we all know who our fathers are.' He paused, twisted his neck to the left, then to the right, then left again, where Abudu Olwit sat. He looked pointedly at Olwit and for a few moments their eyes locked. Olwit's face was calm and his jaw was set. Some of the audience sniggered. Others looked down. Yet others grumbled loudly. 'I am not talking about any particular person when I say that sometimes I wonder whether we all know who our fathers are or where they come from. What I

154

am saying is that what you can do for people can be seen from what your own parents did for people. As you all know, the guinea fowl can only be as bald as its forbears, no more.' Adoli-Awal's supporters cheered him, while the rest of the audience stayed silent. Then Adoli-Awal invited his mother to stand up. '*Imat Geto, yaa malo*!' he said (*Imat* Geto, stand up!). His mother, seated almost directly in front of him, got slowly, painfully up, supporting her age-weakened frame on a long, well-worn walking stick. 'Turn round and let everybody see you,' he commanded. *Imat* Geto turned and faced the audience. 'This is my mother,' Adoli-Awal told the gathering, proudly. 'Those of you who are her agemates know what she was as a girl and as a young woman. She brought shame neither to her family nor to her husband, my father. I am proud of her.' He beckoned to *Imat* Geto to sit down. She resumed her place on a large papyrus mat. 'There are some people among us here,' Adoli-Awal went on, ' who would not have the courage to ask their mother to stand up so that they can tell a gathering of people that they are proud of her.' He again looked pointedly at Olwit. Olwit stared coldly back at him.

Adoli-Awal went on to talk about how he first became a member of parliament before he was thirty, and about how he had brought pride to the people of Teboke by getting into parliament at such a young age. He also talked about how he had been active in the struggle to throw Major General Idi off the seat of power, and how he had always had the people of Teboke at heart.

Some of the audience grumbled.

'I have big plans for Teboke,' Adoli-Awal went on. 'I have bigger plans than constructing borehole pumps and water dams. That is why I want you to return me to parliament.' Then he went on to compare himself with an old potter, whose experience ensured that the pots he made would not crack while being baked. Then he resumed his seat.

The next candidate to be invited to speak was Luka Apel. The moment Luka Apel got up, a man in the audience put up his hand and asked him, 'I did not understand your name. What did you say your name was?' The question asker was young and was unsteady on his feet with drink.

'Apel. Luka Apel,' the candidate responded, soberly.

'*Apele*?' the drunken man asked. (A sissy?)

The audience roared with laughter. Some made half-hearted attempts to reprimand him.

'The man says his name is *apele*!' the drunkard shouted. 'What sort of name is that?'

The audience roared with laughter again.

Luka Apel was teased, ridiculed and heckled until, in frustration, he decided to resume his seat, cradling his face between his hands.

Then it was Abudu Olwit's turn to speak.

'The people of Teboke,' he said, 'you all know who I am. I grew up among you, went to Makerere University, and came back here to live among you. I am saying that I came back to live among you not because I live here in Teboke but because I worked at Alaro Prison Farm for some time, and Alaro Prison Farm is not very far from here. And if it had not been for my arrest and jailing, I would still be at Alaro Prison Farm.' He cleared his throat. 'My mother is not here right now. And my father was not a chief like other people's fathers. Yet–'

'Who was your father?' someone in the audience shouted.

'Shut up!' somebody else shouted back.

Some people laughed. Some sniggered. Some looked down.

Abudu Olwit ignored the question about his father's identity.

'I am still young,' Olwit continued, 'yet I do not hide myself when other people are suffering, the way some men hide themselves in Kampala when there is any kind of trouble at all in Teboke and other places.' He lifted his eyes to the mango leaves over his head. Then he brought them down and looked briefly at Adoli-Awal. Their eyes locked. He turned his attention back to the audience after that. 'As I told you, I am still young. As you can see for yourselves. But some of us, since they look younger than they should because of good eating and dyeing their hair, seem unable to think of anything besides dancing at beer gatherings and sleeping with other people's wives.' Then he looked pointedly at the Honourable Adoli-Awal. Abudu Olwit's supporters clapped and cheered. 'A chick that will grow up into a cock can be seen at its hatching,' he went on. 'I am

156

still only a chick. I will grow up into a cock that you will all be proud of.'

Then Abudu Olwit talked about the help he gave to the people of Teboke when they were struck by famine. He talked about the boreholes and dams that 'he' had sunk. He said that what he needed now was support from the Teboke people so that he could be in a position to help them even better. That was the main reason why he wanted the people gathered under the mango trees to vote for him – not so that he could get fat on money from parliament. Then he resumed his seat.

When the Teboke campaign meeting ended the candidates and their campaign managers went their separate ways, without so much as nodding in recognition to each other, much less shaking hands or bidding each other farewell.

***

To-date the police do not know who cast that first stone. That first stone that struck Saida Acola, Abudu Olwit's wife, on the back of the head and sent her sprawling to the ground, off her chair cushioned in maroon leather. That stone that almost caused deaths. And today the people of Alemi, Teboke, Cegere and the neighbouring villages talk about the person they think did it only in whispers. And also about the people they think killed Adoli-Awal's mother, *Imat* Geto.

The hostility and tension between Mike Adoli-Awal and Abudu Olwit had been escalating by the day. Things had worsened to the point where some of their supporters did not talk to each other any more.

Luka Apel had dropped out of the contest. He felt that however much time, energy and money he expended on his efforts to make himself acceptable, the people of Ayer constituency would never quite see him as one of them. So one day, before many people had woken up, he had driven his silver Mazda hatchback through Okole swamp and headed back to Kampala.

That had left only Mike Adoli-Awal and Abudu Olwit in the fight for parliament. And that fight had been nasty.

The campaign meeting that was to be the last – though it had not been scheduled to be the last – took place at Alemi. It was held at the

the Alemi sub-county headquarters. The meeting attracted a large gathering. Odwong, Abudu Olwit's maternal uncle, was there. And so were Adoli-Awal's mother, *Imat* Geto, and Abudu Olwit's mother, Alicinora. Saida Acola was there too, brought along by her own husband.

The Honourable Adoli-Awal was the first to speak. When he got up to speak he did not even glance at Abudu Olwit. The first thing he did was to refer to 'rumours he had heard' about what Abudu Olwit and his agents had been saying about him. One of the rumours, he said, was that he had been the one behind Olwit's recent arrest and imprisonment.

'You were!' somebody in the audience yelled.

'I was not!' Mike Adoli-Awal yelled back, firmly.

'Anyone who thinks that I am the one who caused Olwit's arrest and imprisonment is free to provide the proof – even here.' He paused and swept his eyes around the audience.

Olwit turned to look at him. His eyes were slitted and a strange light danced in them. The man has me arrested and jailed, he pondered, and then he goes ahead to deny it. In my presence.

'Any one of you who thinks that the rumour about my causing Olwit's arrest and imprisonment is true can come up here and say it aloud.' He paused. 'I am waiting.'

He stood around for a few moments, waiting to be publicly accused. No-one came up. 'You see,' he went on, ' I know that this is just a lie spread around by someone who does not have large enough balls to dare face me.'

Some members of the audience laughed. Others winced. Others grumbled.

The man thinks he can do this to me and get away with it, Abudu Olwit thought. Let us wait and see. When it comes my turn to speak I will ask him to tell us who he thinks was responsible for my arrest and imprisonment and see how he responds to that.

'There was a time,' Mike Adoli-Awal went on, 'when I thought that at gatherings such as this one people would be asking me more useful questions than about the arrest of someone whose father is not even known.'

158

It was upon Adoli-Awal saying this that the trouble began. At least, when the people of Ayer constituency think back to the campaign, that is the moment they trace the beginning of the trouble to.

The moment the Honourable Mike Adoli-Awal hinted at Abudu Olwit's uncertain paternity, Olwit's mother, Alicinora, rose up and spoke. '*En Olwit be papere dang tye ba*!' she announced. (But Olwit too has a father!).

'Who is his father?' Mike Adoli-Awal asked. 'Can you tell us what his name is? And where he is? And where he comes from?'

A loud grumbling arose from among the audience, but it was at first difficult to discern what it portended. It rose and swelled like a wave, menacing in its mute intensity. Soon, however, a clear voice arose from the grumbling. The voice belonged to Abudu Olwit's uncle, Odwong.

'Adoli-Awal,' he shouted, 'you have insulted us and Olwit enough. A man of your age should have learnt now that abuse has little value.'

A number of voices came up to support Odwong. Some urged moderation in the campaign. Others asserted that they were fed up with Adoli-Awal, that they wanted somebody else to represent them in parliament.

The Honourable Adoli-Awal raised up his hand. The audience fell silent. 'I know some of you think I should not have been standing again,' he said.

'Yes!' some of the audience yelled.

'No!' yelled others.

'To those who think that I should not have been standing again, I want to say this: Even if I were to give up my parliamentary seat, I would surrender it to someone whose father we all know, but not somebody about whose father some people say he is this one and other people say he is that one.'

That was when the stone came floating through the air. Nobody really knows whether it was intended for her. Well, the stone came floating through the air and someone shouted: 'Saida, look out!' Instead Saida Acola looked up and the stone hit her squarely on the forehead, sending her sprawling to the ground. A jet of blood shot out of the spot the stone had made contact with.

159

'They have killed Olwit's wife!' a woman screamed.

To-date no-one is certain about how the events that followed unfolded. Some say that someone grabbed a chair and threw it at Mike Adoli-Awal. Others say that the folding chair was actually meant for Abudu Olwit, but instead it missed its target and struck Mike Adoli-Awal on the chest. The confusion that ensued, however, was unparallelled in Alemi's post-colonial history. The fight that broke out instantly engulfed the whole meeting place, leaving many people with split lips, broken heads and broken bones. Abudu Olwit was one of the very first victims of the melee. He was trampled into a coma and left lying a short distance away from his silver-grey Toyota Corona saloon. When his supporters saw him lying there, they thought he was dead. So they sought out his rival, Mike Adoli-Awal. By now Saida Acola had sat up, and was looking dazedly at the events taking place around her, part of her gleaming hair matted with congealed blood.

The Honourable Adoli-Awal had just got into his Toyota Landcruiser when the main body of Abudu Olwit's supporters arrived at the car.

'Catch him!' one of them shouted.

'Burn the car!' another screamed.

As Adoli-Awal sped off, they hurled stones at the vehicle, smashing its rear window. He drove off in the direction of Teboke, following the route along which the vengeance ghosts had been chased when famine had struck Teboke barely three years earlier.

As he drove furiously away, frantic and panic-stricken, Adoli-Awal constantly glanced at his rear-view mirror. Somebody had got behind the wheel of Abudu Olwit's car and was giving furious chase. Others were chasing him on motorcycles, on bicycles, even on foot. Adoli-Awal knew that none of the machines chasing him was any match for his infinitely more powerful car. His only worry was, however, that he might find the section of the road at Abari, five miles ahead, flooded with water, since it had rained the whole night the previous day. Sometimes the flooding was so bad that the road became impassable. There was no knowing what Abudu Olwit's supporters would do to him or his car if they found him stuck there.

160

***

It was only much later that *Imat* Geto was discovered. She was lying dishevelled in her expensive new *gomici* behind the school latrine, her withered skin dry and scaly like a lizard's. Her eyes were wide open, staring inscrutable and vacuous at the dark sky roiling with impending rain. When *Imat* Geto's body was picked up off the ground, her head hung limp and helpless as that of a dead turkey. Her neck had been brutally broken.

Epilogue

Mayhem in Apac

Violence flared up yesterday at a campaign meeting at Alemi, Apac district, northern Uganda. The violence marred the final lap in the race for the Ayer constituency parliamentary seat, a contest pitting veteran politician and incumbent Mike Adoli-Awal against newcomer Abudu Olwit. The violence was sparked off by an insult that the incumbent directed at Abudu Olwit and that called Olwit's mother's sexual morality into question. The resulting stampede left Abudu Olwit in a coma and set Adoli-Awal to flight in his luxury Toyota Landcruiser. Adoli-Awal could not, however, reach the Lira-Kampala tarmac road because he learnt that the road that led to it, the Teboke-Loro road, had been blocked by Abudu Olwit's supporters, who were baying for his blood. He had to take an alternative road that leads to Apac town. By press time, Adoli-Awal's supporters were still trying to push his car out of a flooded stretch of the road at Ilee, a small trading centre situated a few kilometres to the south-east of Apac town.

The most tragic occurrence at the campaign meeting was, however, the death of Adoli-Awal's mother, *Imat* Geto. Her body was found behind a latrine at the campaign place several hours after the fighting had ceased. The cause of her death was thought to be a broken neck.

On the other hand, reports regarding Adoli-Awal's rival, Abudu Olwit, indicate that he has been admitted to St Paul's Hospital Apicil, and that his condition is stable. His wife, Saida Acola, who had been injured on the head by a stone, was reported to be by his bedside looking a little the worse for wear.

The turn of political events in Ayer constituency seems to indicate that the parliamentary election there will have to be postponed until the two contenders for the parliamentary seat have sorted out their misunderstandings. As of now, that appears to be quite a remote possibility.

The Daily Chronicle, Monday 17 February

Glossary

acoi	a type of beer made from finger millet or sorghum.
akopi	commoner.
Apap	Dad.
aranga	a kind of 'introduction fee' that a man pays for the girl or woman he is marry-ing.
askari	a guard or watchman.
Atat	Grandmother (as a term of address).
Ayaa	Mother (as a term of address).
cede	a word used to express contempt for the person in respect of whom it is used.
catabiket	(corruption of) certificate.
debe	a type of large tin container.
digiri	(corruption of) degree.
dokta	(corruption of) doctor.
gabuna	(corruption of) governor (administra-tor).
gombolola	sub-county.
gomesi/gomici an	ankle-length dress with up-raised shoulders that are very popular in central and south-central Uganda.
icac	a type of plant; it is hard, very black and gnarled, and is used in many Lango traditional ceremonies.
ikoyi	a sheet of cloth wound around the body; it is worn by women.
iponga	a tall, thin plant whose dark-grey bark is used as a binder in house construction.

163

itek	a type of tree that is generally treated with awe; ancestral and other types of spirits are believed to dwell in it.
jago	sub-county chief.
kapten	captain.
kea	bastardisation of KAR (the King's African Rifles), a section of the British colonial army.
kodi	a word used to request permission to enter a house.
karibu	as a response to *kodi,* granting permission.
kwete	a drink made from maize or a mixture of maize and cassava; it is drunk direct from a cup or calabash when it is still sweetish.
leptenan	lieutenant.
mabati	corrugated, galvanised iron sheets.
nget	a short-handled, small-bladed hoe used mainly for digging up cassava tubers and weeding millet, simsim and groundnut crops.
olam	a type of tree with a thick trunk, a spreading crown and very sticky sap.
opica	(corruption of) officer.
onami	(derogatory/neutral) Bantu-speaking peoples. Singular: *anam.*
opobo	a pink plant that grows thin and tall, and that is frequently used as a whip.
otule	a Lango dance; involves singing and blowing animal horns as the dancers jump up and down.
owak	a kind of tree.
pachwett	bastardised form of 'password(s)'.
pici	PC(Provincial Commissioner).
pwoda	a car, especially if it is long and

luxurious; corruption of 'Ford', probably the first car make that the Langi saw.

ugali bread made by adding millet, sorghum or maize flour to boiling water, stirring it and allowing it to set.

wiri a type of alcoholic beverage made from maize flour and granular sugar or molasses. It also serves as the raw material for *arege* production.

www.ingramcontent.com/pod-product-compliance
Lightning Source LLC
Chambersburg PA
CBHW070227030726
47505CB00006B/1860

* 9 7 8 9 9 7 0 0 2 3 4 3 1 *